HILLARY AVIS

A Flock and a Fluke

Clucks and Clues Cozy Mysteries Book Two

Contents

Chapter 1

Saturday before Easter, Day 1

"I don't know why I let you talk me into this," I said over my shoulder to my usually best friend and currently worst enemy, Ruth Chapman. The crowd pressed us forward and I grudgingly dropped my five-dollar bill into the coffee can and collected a paper scroll tied with a yellow ribbon from the table of Girl Scout volunteers who were set up in front of the bank.

Ruth dropped her money in the can, too. Her wild, springy curls danced in the spring breeze as she plucked her own scroll from the table. "Come on—this is exciting! What else do you have to do, anyway?"

I could think about a million better ways to spend a Saturday morning than running around town looking for pieces of plastic, but I chose the most pressing one. "I need to get my egg order ready for the Rx Café. They're planning a big Easter brunch tomorrow and ordered twice as many as usual."

I was new to the egg business. My flock of hens at Lucky Cluck Farm started laying only six weeks ago. While their eggs were beautiful and perfect in my eyes, they were still pullet-sized, about two-thirds the size they'd be at full maturity. But happily, I'd already found a faithful regular customer for them in the small café that was attached to the pharmacy downtown. The little eggs were perfect for scrambles, omelets, and in pancakes and baked goods—plus, I sold them at a discount. I hoped that in the coming months, as the eggs became larger and more uniform in size, the Rx Café's owner, Sara, would raise her egg budget.

"Oh, hush. Sara already got her eggs for today and she won't need more until tomorrow. You have plenty of time." Ruth rolled her eyes at me and nudged me toward the podium that was set up in front of City Hall, right across the street from the Do or Dye, Ruth's bohemian hair salon. The brick building had three front doors because it served as the fire station and sheriff's office, too. Honeytree, Oregon, was too small to have its own police force. Even the mayor was only part-time, and the fire department was all volunteer.

As I leaned to see between the heads of the people in front of me, I spotted Eli Ramirez, the sheriff's chief deputy assigned to this part of the county, doing some crowd control.

"Take a few steps back, now," he said, flashing a grin when he spotted me. I blushed even though I had no real reason to. Eli and I had dated some four decades ago, but life had taken us on different paths in the intervening years. After high school, he'd joined the Marines and I'd opted for a glamorous life in Beverly Hills. Now that I was back in town, he was sure we were meant to be together, but I was pretty sure I was meant to be alone. We compromised by being friends with a dash of flirtation.

Eli's attention turned back to the growing group of towns-people and tourists, all eagerly clutching their beribboned scrolls. "You can stand in the street, folks, but keep the sidewalks clear for pedestrians."

Only in Honeytree was it A-OK to block Main Street in order to announce the rules for a dang Easter Egg Scramble.

"This is silly," I muttered. "What are we waiting for?"

"Pastor Cal and his wife are hiding the treasure eggs," Ruth explained. "They couldn't hide them too early because they didn't want people out hunting before the Scramble officially started. That'd ruin the fun."

The treasure eggs were new this year, or so Ruth had told me. The old Scramble, back when I was a kid and my dad supplied all the Easter eggs to the city, was held in the back garden of the Methodist church. The eggs were real, hardboiled in the school cafeteria, and dyed by the nice ladies in the Friends of the Library. When I was a teen, the Friends switched to plastic eggs with candy inside due to food safety concerns, much to my father's chagrin. But this year, the mayor was taking things to a whole new level.

The kids would still have their plastic-egg Scramble, but now the adults would have one, too. Twenty eggs, hidden around town, were filled with codes that could be redeemed for cash at the bank. Clues to their locations were listed on the scrolls that we all clutched in our hands as we waited for the official word that we could open them and begin the search. The idea was that a yearly treasure hunt would bring some much-needed tourism to our small town and inject a little cash into local business. Judging by the number of unfamiliar faces in the crowd, it had worked.

I spotted Pastor Cal weaving his way toward the podium and breathed a sigh of relief. This would all be over soon.

He cleared his throat, straightened his pale blue tie, and bent over the microphone. "Good morning, all."

"Good morning, Pastor Cal," the crowd chorused, even Ruth.

I elbowed her gently. "He's not *your* pastor."

She looked at me all gooey-eyed. "He's *everyone's* pastor," she said.

Scanning the crowd, I had to admit she was right. All of Honeytree seemed enchanted by the young—well, relatively young—charismatic pastor. There was no shortage of churches in town, but his pews overflowed on Sunday. People hung on his every word. I was sure that had nothing to do with the fact that he looked like Jack Kennedy and was married to a woman who looked like Marilyn but had Jackie's poise and style.

"Amelia's been held up, but we'll start shortly. As soon as she gets here." He smiled broadly, his All-American white teeth glinting in the bright morning, instantly putting me at ease. It was no wonder that support for his mayoral campaign was growing. One could easily imagine him as president, let alone mayor.

A woman leaned between him and the mic. It was the current mayor, Margie Morrow, squeezed into a pink tweed skirt-suit. Her teased, dye-box-red bob quivered as she glared up at him. "I don't think it's necessary to wait on her. She's probably just in the ladies' room. We don't want to hold up the hunt, do we?"

Something in Pastor Cal's expression chilled, although the smile never left his face. "Sure, Marge. Whatever you say."

She shooed him backward a few steps and then turned to face the crowd. "Friends," she said warmly into the microphone, holding out her hands toward us. I snorted. If I knew one thing, it was that Margie Morrow wasn't my friend. Even in high school, when I was a perky cheerleader full of school spirit and she was student council president, we weren't friends.

"Why's Marge-in-Charge trying to be nice?" I asked Ruth under my breath.

"You be nice," Ruth admonished. "At least she's trying."

Margie, having stretched out her dramatic pause long enough that people began murmuring restlessly, continued. "I'm so glad you all came to our little Scramble. In your hands, you hold the key to the treasure…all you need now is a pair of sharp eyes. Searching must be accomplished on foot, please. We don't want reckless drivers tearing around town."

For some reason, it felt like she was talking to me personally. I have a little bit of a reputation for my lead foot. What can I say? I like the feeling of wind in my hair.

"Stay off private property and leave everything as you find it. Only one other rule—conduct yourselves like ladies and gentlemen. If you don't, your prize will be revoked by the sheriff." Margie motioned to Eli, who stepped toward the mic.

"You won't be allowed to redeem your prize code if you've engaged in any unethical behavior. No cheating, stealing, or fighting, please. Remember, this is Honeytree, where life is sweet." He recited the town motto with a hint of irony quirking the corner of his mouth. I might be the only one who spotted it. "I'll be at the bank all day to ensure civility," he added.

An official announcement that there would be no sheriff patrol today? The criminals in town must be rejoicing. It might be time to take my little Porsche convertible out of the barn for some drag racing on the flat stretch of highway in front of my farm. I smirked and looked around to see if anyone else was thinking the same thing, but the crowd seemed more intent on what the mayor would say next.

Margie held up one finger. "Oh, and before we begin, don't forget to vote Morrow for Mayor on May twelfth during our special mayoral election. Every vote counts!" she chirped. Behind her, Pastor Cal opened his mouth, presumably to plug his own campaign, but before he could get in a word, Margie clapped her hands. "On your marks, get set, go!"

A frenzy of chatter broke out. Ruth and I hurriedly untied our ribbons to look at the clues as all those around us did the same. I scanned the sheet of paper as quickly as I could. Each of the twenty eggs had a short, one-line clue. They were divided by color: red eggs were valued at $100, blue eggs at $500, and one golden egg held a code for a whopping $1000.

My eyes nearly popped, and I heard gasps from others in the crowd, too, as they saw the amounts.

"I told you," Ruth said, her eyes dancing with excitement. "This is going to be *fun*."

I skipped the lower-value clues and read the first blue-egg clue aloud. "Near or far, or at the bar, you'll find me where U are." I instantly knew where the egg was hidden. "It's the U-Turn Tavern!"

I grabbed Ruth's handknit cardigan sleeve and ran south down Second Street toward the dusty old cinderblock building with "U-Turn Here" painted in faded letters on the side. The dive bar wasn't called the U-Turn anymore—now it had some other name—but it'd been U-Turn for so long that people still called it that.

To my dismay, about twenty other people had deciphered the clue at the same time and barreled ahead of us. I guess two fifty-something women who eat a lot of apple pie and prefer chatting by a bonfire to doing Pilates aren't exactly Olympic athletes. Ruth and I slowed to a stop and watched the pack of rabid egg hunters scour the building's exterior and the thin strip of landscaping that separated the U-Turn from the highway. Then, a pimply young guy in a saggy gray T-shirt who'd been investigating the gutter downspouts held up a blue egg triumphantly.

"Found it!" he hollered across the parking lot.

There was a lot of muttering and cursing as all of the folks who'd been searching the bushes pulled out their scrolls and tried to decipher the next clue.

"We're not going to win a foot race," I said to Ruth. "We need to be strategic so we're not trying to outpace the Roadrunner. Maybe there'll be less competition for the hundred-dollar eggs."

She nodded, scanning her scroll. "How about this one? It's a red egg. 'Under here, you're without fear. Unless Coach Randall is near.'"

"High school bleachers," I said instantly. I couldn't help darting a glance over my shoulder at Eli, who was strolling from City Hall toward the bank, an amused expression on his face as he watched the Scramble chaos around him. He and I had spent plenty of time making out under those bleachers between classes. Heck, sometimes during classes. The memory was so strong, I could almost taste the Doublemint gum that he always chewed.

Coach Randall never caught us kissing, but we lived in fear of him. With one word, he could kick Eli off the football team for cutting class. One jingle of his keys in the distance, and we were running for our lives. "That's way across town. You couldn't pay me a hundred bucks to run that far—remember, we have to run back, too. Our best bet is to pick the hardest clue and hope nobody else figures it out."

"Cross your fingers the golden egg is hidden closer," Ruth said, grinning. "I bet the gold clue is the toughest one."

I nodded and read the clue aloud. "It ain't over 'til it's over. We've got you covered." Then I laughed. It couldn't be that easy.

"What does it mean?" Ruth's forehead creased. "'It ain't over'? Is that some business that is closed? Or maybe the construction site on D Street? That project is taking forever."

I shook my head as I discreetly checked to see if anyone was heading in the direction I thought the egg was hidden. A couple of groups from the U-Turn Tavern splintered off toward the school, and others, who'd undoubtedly worked out another clue, ran uphill toward the Church of the Everlasting. Of course, Pastor Cal and Amelia had hidden one of the eggs at their home church. But nobody seemed to have solved the golden egg clue—yet.

"'We've got you covered,'" Ruth mused. "That could refer to insurance coverage."

"Hey!" A skinny woman with dark hair in two long, equally skinny braids waved her arms and called to her friend across the street. "This lady says there's one at the insurance place!" The two of them made a mad dash down the street toward the blue building with striped awnings that advertised the Honeytree slogan with a twist: "Life is Sweet…When You're Insured."

"I don't want people to see where we're going," I murmured, and Ruth gave a quick nod.

"I give up! Let's go get a milkshake," she said, her tone dejected but her voice loud enough to carry down the block. She crammed her scroll in the back pocket of her jeans. I grinned and did the same with my clues. Those years Ruth spent onstage doing school plays hadn't gone to waste.

Arm-in-arm, we strolled down the block and turned onto

the highway like we were going to follow it to the diner for a bite to eat. But we didn't. As soon as we were far enough that it was clear nobody was watching us, I pulled Ruth onto the side street by the library.

I kept my voice low even though the street was empty, quickening my pace as we got closer to where I knew the egg was hidden. "You know how they moved the covered bridge over here?" The historic wooden bridge had once been designed for horse carts in its youth, and then even cars and log trucks trundled across one at a time, when we were kids. Now deeming it structurally unsound for loads that heavy, the city council had voted to move the bridge for use as a pedestrian walkway between the library and the public baseball field where a small creek divided the two properties.

Ruth nodded. "The egg can't be there, though. The bridge is closed until they build the on-ramps."

"Exactly! It ain't over—over the creek—until it's over. Until the construction is finished," I explained.

"Then it says, 'We've got you covered.' I guess that's just because it's a covered bridge?"

"Maybe. Or maybe it's another clue to where the egg is hidden."

I glanced over my shoulder as we entered the library parking lot. Nobody was following us, but it was only a matter of time until someone else deciphered the clue. We needed to work fast if we were going to uncover that egg. I broke into a jog and Ruth followed me, one arm clamped over her chest so her ample assets wouldn't smack her in the chin.

"Oh no," Ruth wailed as we neared the bridge. We halted, dismayed by the scene in front of us. The bridge was totally cordoned off with chain link fencing. Signs posted on it said,

"Stay Out — Under Construction — Trespassers Prosecuted." There was no way to reach any part of the structure without disobeying the signs, and I had a feeling that disobeying city signage fell under Marge Morrow's definition of uncivilized behavior.

"Maybe it *is* at the insurance office," Ruth mused.

"No." I shook my head stubbornly, narrowing my eyes as I scanned the area. "It has to be here somewhere."

I began searching the bottom of the fence line where clumps of Bermuda grass had grown up around some of the posts. It was temporary fencing, but like all the other construction projects in town, the bridge walkway build had been delayed due to heavy spring rains. The breeze whipped up again, swirling my blonde-and-silver ponytail and pushing a few dark, fluffy clouds over the sun. The weather could change so quickly this time of year—sometimes it seemed we got four seasons per day. A couple of warning drops fell onto my back.

"Oregon liquid sunshine," Ruth remarked, stooping beside me to join me in my search. "We better find this egg before it opens up, or we'll be running for cover."

I stood up abruptly. "We're looking in the wrong place."

"How do you know?"

"'We've got you covered.' We're not covered here. We can't go on the bridge to get out of the rain, so where could we go?"

"The library?" Ruth suggested.

"No—the clue is definitely pointing to the bridge. But if we can't go *on* the bridge, it can still cover us!"

Ruth frowned at me and shook her head. "I don't understand. If we're not under the roof, how can it cover us?"

"Underneath." I pointed ten yards away to the leafy under-brush along the creek bank, where a narrow trail led down to

10

the water. It was mostly traveled by deer, but on hot summer afternoons the neighborhood children would use it to cool off by wading in the shallow creek. "We're going to have to get our feet a little wet."

Ruth looked down at her own feet, encased in a well-worn pair of shearling boots. It might be springtime, but that didn't mean it was warm out. Then she looked back at me. "Uh-uh. I don't care how much money is inside that egg—I'm not putting my feet in that ice water."

I looked back at the library parking lot and beyond it to the side street that led off the highway. In the distance, a couple of small figures moved toward us and I could hear the sound of raised voices, even though I couldn't make out exactly what they were saying. "They're catching up. It's now or never, Ruth!"

She crossed her arms and shook her head so hard that her feather earrings fluttered. "Never. If you want to go swimming, that egg is all yours."

I shrugged and swiftly moved to the narrow entrance, parting the vine maple leaves and ducking under a few blackberry brambles that had grown across the narrow path. I half-ran, half-slid down to the creek itself. I sat down to tug off my hiking boots—I'd worn my good shoes to town instead of the grubby barn shoes I usually wore around Lucky Cluck Farm—and left them creekside with my purse, splashing my way toward the underside of the covered bridge.

The creek was clear and, as Ruth predicted, full of frigid snowmelt from the Cascades. My feet burned with the cold as I picked my way over the rocks, coming to a halt in the shadow that the bridge cast over the creek. The old wooden bridge now rested on new steel supports, held up on either side of the creek by concrete pylons. At the base of each pylon, a small sandy bar had formed, kind of a miniature beach. I leaped to the nearest one, dancing as my toes—bright red from the cold—pinged with the pain of the temperature change, and searched the creek bank and bridge for signs of the egg.

The sun emerged briefly from behind a cloud, and I caught sight of a glint of gold in the bushes directly opposite me.

"Leona! They're coming!" I heard Ruth's urgent cry from above, and the sound of crashing through the brush. Without thinking, I plunged across the creek, sinking up to my thighs in the rushing water. It was like moving through liquid lead, but I made it to the other side of the water, freezing, dripping, and with adrenaline ringing in my ears.

Cheese and rice, all this for a plastic egg.

I dropped to my knees and scrabbled under the bush for the prize. My hand closed on it—and something else. I fell back on my butt, the golden egg in hand, and then leaned forward to see if I had felt what I thought I'd felt.

Fingers.

A woman's hand, neatly manicured with light pink polish, the long delicate fingers slightly blue at the tips. It was attached to a beautiful, porcelain arm with a pale blue, organdy sleeve. I followed it with dread to the other side of the bush where, sprawled out, eyes staring up at a patch of sky as blue as her dress, was a woman I recognized.

It was Amelia Goodbody, Pastor Cal's wife. And she was definitely, one hundred percent dead.

Chapter 2

"Help! Someone!" I yelled. Two searchers who'd made it to the creek and were shucking their shoes stopped and looked up at me in surprise. I stood up and waved. "Hey! Get help! Someone's hurt!"

They froze and then looked at each other and exchanged a few words. One of them, a bearded man in a bright blue hoodie who I recognized as one of the local gas station attendants, squinted at me across the creek. "You're just trying to keep us away from the gold egg, lady. We know it's around here somewhere, and we deserve it as much as you do. You take that side, we'll take this one."

"This is an emergency, you idiots. I just found a dead woman. So could you please either help me or call someone who can?"

"Leona?" Ruth's question filtered through the brush and across the water. "Are you OK?"

I cupped my hands to my mouth. All those years of cheerleading practice had better pay off like Ruth's acting roles had earlier. "I found a body!" Pause. Breath. "Other side of the creek!" Shorter pause, breath. "Call Eli!" I bellowed through my makeshift megaphone.

I turned back to Amelia beside me and felt for a pulse. I don't know why—her blue lips and fingers, her staring eyes, and the temperature of her skin told me what I already knew, that she was dead—but I guess I was hoping for an Easter miracle.

No such luck. In spite of the fact that she didn't appear injured in any way—there wasn't even a smudge on her pretty blue dress—she wasn't going to rise from the dead.

The idiots across the stream were still frozen and staring at me. Useless. I noticed a basket beside Amelia, empty of whatever it had held. It looked like she had keeled over just as she was hiding the golden egg. I slipped the egg into my cargo pocket so it wouldn't get lost and reached to close her eyes. It was all I could do for her. It was clearly too late for CPR.

I heard sirens in the distance. Ruth had come through. Minutes that felt like months later, a team of two paramedics burst out of the brush behind me, kneeling immediately at Amelia's side. They took her vitals—which obviously weren't good; I could have told them that—and then one crew member began CPR even though, as I'd determined, it was clearly useless. It must be protocol. I swallowed hard.

"You can go wait by the truck for the sheriff," the second paramedic said gently, touching my arm. Her brown eyes were sympathetic, but she didn't have much time to spend on me and quickly turned her attention back to her partner and Amelia.

I stood and backed down the bank to the creek. "I'll be over by the library," I said. "If the sheriff is looking for me."

I waded back across the creek, ignoring the looky-loo hoodie boys, and collected my purse and hiking boots from the rock by the creek before scrabbling my way up the steep dirt path. Ruth met me at the top of the creek bank, gnawing her lip worriedly.

"Are you OK? What's going on over there?"

Another lump grew in my throat. "Everything's fine," I

croaked. "I mean, the paramedics came. They have her."

"Who?" Ruth asked urgently, and then her eyes clouded with concern as she reached out to touch my goose-pimpled forearm. "Oh, Leona, you're shaking! You must be drenched to the skin! Come on, let's get you warm."

She bustled me over to the library parking lot where a marked sheriff's SUV was pulling up. Eli got out, his face somber, and immediately went around to the back of the rig and pulled out one of those silver mylar blankets from his emergency kit. He wrapped it around me like foil around a baked potato, tucking it in around the edges, clucking like a mother hen. "Did you fall? Are you hurt? I want EMS to take a look at you."

"Stop! I'm fine!" I protested. "I just want to go home."

He sighed. "You can't just yet. Take a minute inside the library and warm up before I record your statement. I need to go check on the scene anyway."

"Well, you'd better drive around. The creek's pretty high," I said, my teeth chattering even though the rest of me was starting to heat up inside my tin-foil cocoon.

"Come on." Ruth urged me toward the library, and I nodded and followed her across the small parking lot and up the steps to the main entrance.

I could think of few places in Honeytree more welcoming than our little library, where I'd spend nearly every day after school until my mother finished her secretarial job at the law office downtown. The librarian, Lucy Patrick, had been like a second mother to me. She didn't fuss over me or baby me, but she always made sure I had a comfortable seat and a good book to keep me company on rainy afternoons. Though Lucy Patrick was long retired, it still smelled like her inside the building, like vanilla and paper and dried lavender. The most comforting smell in the world.

It wasn't until Ruth and I settled on a bench in the lobby that she asked me what I'd seen. Who I'd found.

"Amelia," I said.

Ruth gasped. "Oh no! Is she OK?"

Denial is a powerful thing. Ruth knew I'd found a body. She'd called in the body. And still she was hoping Amelia was OK. I shook my head.

"What happened—could you tell if she was hurt?"

Two women dressed in raincoats stepped into the lobby, huddling their highlighted heads together like hens on a roost as they pressed their faces to the window. I waited for them to go into the library before I answered Ruth, but instead they stayed near the display case by the front entrance, talking and glancing out every so often at the parking lot and the covered bridge beyond. I could hear their chatter even across the lobby.

"Do you think they'll cancel the whole Scramble?"

"No—how can they? At least half the eggs have been found."

I fingered the egg that was straining the limits of my cargo pocket. A thousand dollars, plucked from a dead woman's fingers.

"I heard it was Mrs. Goodbody," one of them said to the other. "She just collapsed or something."

"Did she?" Ruth whispered to me.

I shrugged, the mylar blanket crinkling. The sound caught the attention of the twittering duo, who wheeled and descended on us, abandoning their post at the window.

"Do you know what happened? Were you there?" They clustered around me, their faces sympathetic above their loud coats, one striped and one flowered. Now that they were closer,

I could tell they were related. Sisters, maybe, or best friends so long that they might as well be sisters.

"She found the body," Ruth said, putting her arm around me protectively.

Striped Raincoat clucked her tongue. "You poor thing. So… was it Amelia? I heard it was Amelia."

I didn't want to answer. Maybe I was in denial, too. It felt like if I spoke it aloud to these two women it would become real—make that three. Another woman with the same blonde highlights but wearing a solid-pink raincoat joined them.

"What's going on? Is she OK?" The woman, who I vaguely recognized as a checker at the grocery store, leaned to get a better look at me in my silver blanket.

Flowered Raincoat filled her in. "She found a dead body in the creek."

The woman's jaw dropped, and she stared at me with new curiosity.

"Amelia wasn't in the creek," I said quietly.

"See, I told you it was Mrs. Goodbody. I knew something was up with her this morning. Our table was next to theirs at breakfast and she was not looking good. She was sweating like a pig and kept running to the restroom." Flowered Raincoat nodded smugly.

"Pregnant?" Pink Raincoat asked.

"I doubt it. Have you seen her waistline? It's as narrow as a swan's neck."

"Maybe she ate a bad egg."

The three women giggled, and I felt my cheeks turn hot. There were only two places in town that served breakfast, the diner and the Rx Café. If they were talking about the latter, they were talking about *my* eggs. And my eggs definitely weren't

17

bad.

I opened my mouth to wipe the silly, smug expressions off their faces, but Ruth seemed to know what I was thinking. She elbowed me and shook her head, mouthing the word 'no' silently. For once, I listened to her.

"Hey, Irene!" Striped Raincoat waved to Irene Wertheimer, who was heading into the library with her walker. Irene was one of the Friends of the Library who'd dyed eggs when I was a child. Though she was pushing ninety now, she was still an active member and had likely spent the past week stuffing plastic eggs with stickers and temporary tattoos—or whatever was allowed these days now that jellybeans had been prohibited along with real eggs and common sense. "You'll never guess what happened!"

Irene shuffled over to join us, the tennis balls on the back legs of her walker hissing on the lobby carpet. When she spotted me all wrapped up like a tinseled tree, her face lit up. She was always happy to be on the front lines of any town gossip. "Are you hurt, dear?" she asked, picking up her glasses from the chain around her neck to peer at me. She clearly hoped so.

"I hate to disappoint you, but no. I just got a little wet in the creek." Understatement of the day. Even my undies were wet now that the water had seeped all the way up my pant legs.

"Guess what!" Flowered Raincoat could barely contain her excitement. "Amelia Goodbody's dead! She ate some bad eggs at the Rx Café and just keeled over!"

Fury balled in the pit of my stomach. She *really* didn't need to bring my eggs into it.

"Oh my word." Irene shook her head, her bright eyes snapping under her plastic bonnet. "How terrible. What a blow for Pastor Goodbody."

Pink Raincoat gasped. "Does he even know?"

The Raincoats looked at each other, their mouths grim under their matching nude lip gloss. "We have to go and tell him! Maybe he ate the same thing."

"What did she order?" I blurted out. I stood up and let the emergency blanket fall to the floor. The Raincoats stared at me and even Irene raised her drawn-on eyebrows. "At breakfast. Did you even see what she ordered? Maybe she had pancakes. Maybe she had biscuits and gravy."

"A woman died. Have a little respect," Flowered Raincoat said, frowning. "What she ordered isn't really relevant."

I was really beginning to dislike her.

"It's not," Ruth said, standing up and taking my elbow to steer me away from them.

"It *is* relevant if they're going to blame it on my eggs!" I said hotly, pulling my arm away from her. "She could have eaten anything!"

Irene put her glasses on again. "*Your* eggs? Did you cook breakfast for Mrs. Goodbody this morning?"

If the Raincoats leaned any closer, I was going to pop them in their big mouths.

"Eli's here," Ruth said quickly. "Don't do anything you'll regret. Take a deep breath, find your center. This is all going to get sorted out."

I shrugged at the four women and turned my back on them to follow Ruth toward the entrance where Eli stood, waiting. Behind me, I heard them whispering.

"The sheriff's taking her statement!"

"*She* made Amelia's breakfast!"

"I know, can you believe it?"

"What do you think she had against her?"

"Maybe she had a thing for the pastor."
"Well, who doesn't."
Giggles.

Chapter 3

"Ruth, do you mind waiting on the other side of the lobby until we're done?" Eli said. He had his clipboard out to take my statement, and he tapped his pen against it impatiently. "I need to interview you separately."

"We were together the whole time!" Ruth protested, but I shook my head.

"No, we weren't. Go. I'll be fine." My voice wobbled on the last word, and she still looked worried. "Really, I will."

She squeezed my hand. "Take a deep breath and find your center. I'll be right there if you need me." She retreated to the far side of the lobby where the raincoat ladies were still having a conference. I hoped Ruth's proximity would dampen their enthusiasm for gossip. Probably not, though—Ruth's chair at the Do or Dye was pretty much gossip central, and judging by their matching, very nice highlights, they'd all sat there a time or two.

I sighed, and Eli dropped his voice so only I could hear. "Really, are you OK?"

"Does it matter?" I asked. Just his question made a whole flood of emotions rise in my chest. You know how it is when you scrape your knee and you don't cry until someone asks you about it? This was like that. And I didn't like it. I motioned to his recorder. "Turn it on."

"I'll be jotting some notes, too, but don't let that distract you," he said. I took a deep breath, found my center as Ruth so obnoxiously suggested, and rattled off as much as I could remember about solving the golden egg clue, getting wet in the creek, and finding Amelia Goodbody laid out on the opposite side.

"Was there anyone else around?" he asked when I'd finished.

"Just the idiots in the blue hoodies, but they came after I found her. I didn't see anyone else." My breath caught. "Why, do you think someone did this to her?" The question sounded stupid coming out of my mouth, but I really hadn't thought about that possibility. My adrenaline was so high after I found her that I hadn't considered what *had* happened.

"You know I can't say at this point in an investigation." He shut off the recorder and put it away. "If you remember anything else…"

"I'll call you," I finished glumly.

"Don't sound so excited about it." The corners of his eyes crinkled, and I couldn't help returning his smile. Eli always managed to break down my defenses.

"Good luck with your investigation," I said, glancing over to the cluster of women by Ruth. They were all staring at us expectantly, like I was going to produce a murder weapon as easily as a magician pulling a rabbit out of a hat. Just because I was unlucky enough to solve the golden egg clue before anyone else meant I'd forever be painted by my brush with Amelia's death. How would they like it if the tables were turned?

That gave me an idea. I turned to Eli. "One of them saw Amelia this morning and said she looked ill. The one in the flowered coat."

Eli's face brightened. "Thanks for the lead!" He headed toward them and I took the opportunity to wave to Ruth, ditch the foil blanket in the lobby trashcan, and duck out the back exit. I speed-walked the four blocks back to the Do or Dye, where I'd parked in the side lot, hoping the whole time that nobody would look at me and think I peed my pants. I breathed a sigh of relief when my crotchety Suburban started up right away, and I headed out of town toward home.

When I hit the Flats—in record time, since I knew Eli wasn't on highway patrol—the Suburban's heater had warmed my chilled legs and the drive had soothed my frazzled nerves. I smiled when I saw the familiar, hand-painted sign at the end of my driveway.

Lucky Cluck Farm. My farm.

I turned down the freshly graveled driveway, paid for by my recent pullet-egg sales, that ran through the apple orchard I'd inherited when I bought the place. The trees were just coming into bloom, with more of their pink-and-white blossoms unfurling every day. This year's wet spring promised a bumper apple crop.

The driveway led to the shabby yellow cottage I called home. Just beyond it stood an aging barn that I used as a workshop, garage, and occasional chicken-quarantine unit. And across the driveway from the house was my pride and joy, the heart of Lucky Cluck Farm—my glorious chicken coop. It was so big and deluxe that Eli called it a chicken palace. I'd built it in the fall with help from my friends, and now it was paying dividends in the form of happy, healthy chickens and a cluckload of eggs every day.

It was a good thing, too, because the Rx Café's order for tomorrow was so big that I'd need every egg to fill it. I went straight from the car to the coop to collect any that had been laid while I was in town. My flock chattered with excitement when I approached and a mass of hens swarmed toward the wire at the end of the run, hoping that I'd throw a handful of treats.

"Not this time, girls," I said, grabbing a wire basket from a hook on the side of the coop. I opened the door that allowed me access to the back of the nest boxes, and a wave of satisfaction washed over me when I saw that nearly a dozen more eggs had been laid.

Ten of them were the smooth, brown eggs I expected from my flock, but one was a surprising light aqua. I'd planned my operation to include only one type of hen, a super-productive commercial laying breed, but the hatchery had sent me an extra handful of "packing-peanut" chicks along with my layers, so I had several oddballs. This included a few so-called Easter Eggers that laid colorful eggs. I wouldn't include the blue egg in the Rx Café's order, but it was surprisingly fun to find colored eggs in the mix.

"Thank you!" I said out of habit, even though I knew the chickens didn't care. I really was thankful. My flock was young, but they were already productive layers and I was depending on the income to keep the farm afloat. My retirement plan rested on the tiny shoulders of my feathered friends.

Did chickens even have shoulders?

I grinned at the thought as I watched them eagerly press against the wire. No matter how much I fed them, they always acted like they were starving. "I'll be back later with snacks," I promised, and gingerly carried the basket of eggs into the house. I left them on the counter and shucked my damp cargo pants in favor of some dry overalls before I tackled the order.

I had a few things to do before the eggs were ready for delivery. Oregon law required that I wash, label, and store the eggs in a particular way to sell to restaurants and stores. While I kept eggs for my own consumption on the counter, unwashed, because the natural "bloom" on the surface kept them from spoiling, I thoroughly washed the eggs I sold in a bleach solution and kept in a second fridge on the back porch to hold them. Right now, that fridge was full to bursting, just in time for Easter brunch at the Rx Café.

I set to work and within a couple of hours, I'd washed the new eggs, labeled the cartons, and assembled the entire order. I gingerly carried a cooler of cartons out to the car and drove achingly slowly through the Curves so I wouldn't risk bashing the whole order against the sides of the Suburban and destroying all my—and my hens'—hard work. These eggs might as well be gold.

Speaking of which, the golden egg from this morning was still in my pants pocket on the floor of the bathroom, I remembered as I steered the car carefully through town, on high alert in case Scramblers were still out looking for the last remaining eggs. I made a mental note to take the egg out before it went through the wash and destroyed the prize code.

When I pulled up in front of the Rx Café, I was shocked to see that the tiny restaurant was empty of customers. I'd expected it would be packed, given the Scramble crowd and the fact that it was just after noon on a Saturday, prime time for the little café's breakfast and lunch menu.

I took half the eggs—all I could carry in one trip—through the front door and saw only one table was full. Preston Gilford had papers spread out and was on the phone with someone while he sipped his coffee. I had a sinking feeling that I knew what he was talking about—he was Pastor Cal's campaign manager and was probably under pressure to cancel or reschedule the week's appearances in light of Amelia's death.

I made my way to the counter and a petite, olive-skinned woman with cropped black hair motioned for me to come behind the counter into the open kitchen. Sara, the owner and chef here at the Rx Café. She wore a black-and-white striped apron over her black linen button-down shirt, the sleeves of which were rolled up to reveal a proliferation of tattoos on both arms. She took the eggs from me and set them on the counter.

"Lunch rush is over already?" I asked.

"If there was one." Sara grimaced. "There's a rumor floating around that Amelia Goodbody got food poisoning at breakfast. It's been deserted in here since word got out that she died. They think she got salmonella from the eggs."

"Did she even eat eggs?" I crossed my fingers behind my back, hoping she'd ordered the biscuits and gravy.

Sara nodded. "Three, scrambled. I remember because she specifically said not to bring any potatoes or toast because she's doing some low-carb diet. All she had was eggs."

Of course. My eggs. I had a bad feeling that this problem wasn't just going to go away.

"Hopefully they'll get over it," I said, feeling a little sick myself. "Even if she ate bad eggs, salmonella takes hours to make you sick. You don't just keel over. Everyone knows that."

"Do they, though?" Sara motioned to the deserted café. "It doesn't seem like they know that to me."

"I'll go grab the rest of your order," I said, eager for a breath of fresh air outside, and started to head toward the door.

Sara caught my arm. "No, don't. I'm sorry, Leona—I have to

26

cancel the order. The only way I'm going to make back today's earnings is if I totally change the brunch menu tomorrow. It's going to be all waffles and pancakes."

"Those take eggs, too!" I protested, panic rising in my chest. "Waffles use a ton of eggs."

"I already placed a new order with the grocery store." She bit her lower lip apologetically.

"You're paying retail for eggs?! I'm charging you half of wholesale, Sara—you're going to destroy your profit margins if you switch to grocery store eggs!" My voice rose until even Preston took notice, setting down his phone and rising to his feet.

"Are we having a problem, ladies?" He ran a hand over his hair—he was definitely the kind of guy who got a trim every three weeks—and straightened the lapels of his light gray suit with a habitual movement as he waited for an answer.

"No problem here!" Sara chirped, bustling past me to refill his now-empty coffee cup. "Can I get you anything else?"

He shook his head and sat back down. Punching a button on the screen of his phone, he resumed his conversation. "Sorry about that," he said into the phone. "I just needed to take care of something. I assure you, the pastor will deliver his sermon tomorrow. Amelia would have wanted it that way. Everyone should come out and show their support."

Sara slid the carafe back onto the warmer and rejoined me. "It's just temporary, until this whole thing blows over. In a couple weeks, customers will trickle back in. Then I'll be able to order from you again and it'll be no harm, no foul."

It'd be no harm, no *fowl* if my farm went under, but there was nothing I could do about that. I sighed. "I understand. Hopefully once Amelia's cause of death is determined, the

Honeytree rumor mill will have new grist and they'll leave us out of it!"

"Hear, hear," Sara said, nodding.

I picked up the eggs from the counter and slowly walked out of the café. As I passed Preston, I noticed he'd ended his call. I paused by his table. "I'm so sorry about Amelia," I said. I swallowed. I wanted to tell him that I'd done my best for her, that I'd closed her eyes and stayed with her, but I couldn't figure out a way to do it without it sounding weird. "Give my condolences to the pastor."

Preston flashed me a sad smile. "Why don't you join us for Easter service tomorrow and tell him yourself?"

"I'll think about it," I lied through my teeth on the way out the door.

I had solid plans to sleep in tomorrow, and my closet had solid plans to never hold a dress or a pair of pantyhose again, let alone an Easter bonnet.

Chapter 4

I sat in the Suburban for a few minutes bumping my forehead gently against the steering wheel. What in the world was I going to do with the dozens of eggs I had in the back? Maybe the diner would take them. When I was little, the owner, Ed Wynwood, had bought his eggs from my dad. Maybe the old Landers reputation was still intact at the Greasy Spoon even though it was now run by Ed's son, Ed Junior.

I pulled into the parking lot of the tiny brick building on the edge of town. A giant, spoon-shaped sign on top of the roof was bigger than the building itself. Its bright blue front door still had "Good Eats" painted on it in spindly white letters just as it always had, but someone had definitely repainted it over the years. Though I hadn't been a regular visitor since I moved back to Honeytree, the Greasy Spoon was still known for its cheap coffee that was a decent substitute for battery acid and the prime rib special on Saturday night.

Inside, I spotted Ed Junior working the flat top, his back turned to the door. He was a burly man with a buzzcut, a remnant of his service in Afghanistan. He flipped a row of pancakes, the back of his bright blue T-shirt stained dark with sweat from his efforts, before he looked up and saw me. He raised his spatula in greeting and used it to motion to the single

29

free table.

"I'd say sit anywhere, but you don't have many options," he said. "Jillian will be right with you to get your order." A harried young woman wearing the same blue T-shirt and a server's apron nodded to me from across the tiny restaurant where she was dropping off an armful of plates. The Greasy Spoon only had ten or twelve tables, but in contrast with the tables at the Rx Café, they were all packed, barring the tiny two-person table wedged between the coffee station and a chainsaw sculpture of a bear.

I went to take a seat at the one of the three counter stools instead, brushing past a table of other diners who quieted as I walked by. Word was already out that I was the one who found Amelia's body, I guessed. Their conversation picked back up once I sat down at the counter.

Jillian appeared at my elbow and flipped the coffee cup in front of me right-side-up. "Regular or decaf?"

"No thanks. I just wanted to talk to Ed," I said. Ed grunted and turned back to the grill, deftly chopping up an order of corned beef hash with the hedge of his spatula. A mouthwatering aroma hit my nostrils and my stomach rumbled. "You got a minute?"

Ed scooped the hash onto a plate and handed it to Jillian. "Sure do, for paying customers." He gave me a pointed look.

"Decaf," I said to Jillian, who smiled.

"I'll be right back with your coffee," she promised, and wheeled around to deliver the hash to a table by the window. I was impressed with her calm in the face of the crowded restaurant, given that she was responsible for everything but the cooking. She couldn't be more than nineteen and she had more poise than someone two or three times her age. Me, I realized. She had more poise than me.

"My niece," Ed said gruffly, following my gaze. "She's a hard worker. We're really slammed today."

"I see that. Any chance you're running low on eggs? I have a little egg farm and I've got a few dozen extra." That was an understatement. Ed squinted at me skeptically, his spatula in mid-air, so I played my trump card. "Your dad used to buy eggs from my dad. I'm Leona Landers—Davis now, but Landers was my maiden name."

"You licensed with the state?" he asked. I nodded. "I guess I could use a few more. Give me five dozen."

Well, five dozen was better than nothing. I jumped up just as Jillian returned with a carafe to fill my coffee mug. "Don't worry, I'll pay for that as soon as I get back," I assured her, and bounded out to the parking lot before Ed could change his mind.

When I returned, balancing two flats of eggs, the mood in the busy little restaurant had shifted. All the chattering diners were quiet, their eyes on me as I made my way to the counter. Ed set down his spatula and leaned on the counter, his Basset-hound face serious. Jillian avoided my gaze and darted off to clear a table's dirty dishes. The clatter of the plates echoed in the silence.

"I don't think I'll need those eggs after all," Ed said slowly.

I felt my cheeks flush. Someone had clued him in on what had happened this morning. I tried to keep my voice steady. "These eggs are fresh as they can be, Ed. I just collected them today. I'll even throw in an extra dozen for the trouble."

"I can't have my customers getting sick."

"You know as well as I do that food poisoning doesn't work like that!" I said hotly, blinking back the tears that welled up.

"Amelia might have eaten my eggs, but she didn't drop dead an hour later because of them!"

I heard quiet gasps around me. Even though they'd all been talking about her death—and probably speculating on my involvement—somehow hearing the words come out of my mouth was shocking. What a bunch of hypocrites.

Ed grimaced sympathetically. "I'm sorry—but I just can't take the chance."

"Come on," Jillian said softly beside me, touching my shoulder lightly. "I'll walk you out."

I knew she was trying to save me from further humiliation, this woman young enough to be my daughter. Heck, maybe my granddaughter if I'd come from a different kind of family. I followed her out, nodding thanks as she held the door for me. She tailed me out to my car.

"I don't think any place in town is going to take those," she observed, nodding to the eggs in my hands. Her eyes widened when I opened the back and she saw how many more flats of eggs were in the cooler. I stowed the two flats I carried and turned back to her.

"You can see my dilemma," I said drily.

She nodded, her expression thoughtful. "Listen. If you've got the cold storage, hang on to them for a few days. It'll be a lot easier to sell them once the hubbub has died down and people are eating eggs again. By next week, everybody will have forgotten that they're afraid of salmonella poisoning and will be back to two eggs over easy, white toast, 'browns."

"So you believe me?" I searched her face to see if she was teasing me, but her wide hazel eyes were frank and sympathetic.

"I do. I think you're right—there's no way Amelia Goodbody

died of food poisoning an hour after breakfast. But once you say the word 'food poisoning' in a restaurant, suddenly everyone has stomach cramps. Just bide your time."

"Bide my time," I repeated.

Jillian nodded and tilted her head as she looked at me. "And stop throwing tantrums in public," she added with a grin.

"Did Eli Ramirez tell you to say that?" I asked, only half-joking.

"Came up with it myself. I better get back inside. The customers are revolting." She grinned at her own joke and left me in the parking lot.

I shook my head. Here I was with a car full of eggs that nobody wanted to eat, taking advice from a teenager. But I guess even teenagers are right sometimes. These eggs would be fine in the fridge for weeks. Soon enough, Amelia's death would be explained and my eggs would be exonerated. Then I'd have plenty of eager customers. In fact, I might even sell more eggs from the pent-up demand.

Satisfied, I headed home and unloaded the eggs back into their special fridge on the back porch. I'd just finished the task and gone inside to make myself a very late lunch when I got a call from Ruth.

"You won't believe what's going on in town," she said. I heard the hum of the big hair dryer in her salon in the background, where one of her clients was probably swaddled and reading a magazine.

"I don't know, I'm pretty sure I will. Everyone's talking about how Amelia died because she ate my eggs for breakfast. The Rx canceled my order," I said, my voice cracking like an eggshell.

"Well, there's that." She paused.

There's that? What else was there? "Spit it out, Ruth!"

"You know Aaron?"

I racked my brain, trying to think who she was referring to.

Ruth made a frustrated noise. "Aaron Alpin. The paramedic who gave Amelia CPR?"

I vaguely remembered the pair of first responders. The woman had been kind to me, but the man? I couldn't even conjure up his face, just the top of his head as he leaned over Amelia's body. An involuntary shudder ran through me as I remembered the way she looked there in her pretty blue dress, staring sightless at the sky.

"Leona?"

I jerked to attention, remembering Ruth on the other end of the line. "Sure, the paramedic. What about him?"

"He's sick. Really sick. Sweating, dizzy."

I gasped. "That flowered raincoat lady—she said Amelia had those symptoms at breakfast this morning!"

"Tammy Jenson, yeah. I do her hair. I was thinking the same thing," Ruth said. "Eli took a report from her while I was there, so he knows, too. I talked to him about it when I went to ask him about the ambulance that tore down Main Street. That's when he told me that they took Aaron to the hospital in Pear Grove."

"So Aaron caught whatever she had when he gave her CPR? Some kind of germ?" I frowned. It'd only been about six hours since I found Amelia's body. That wasn't enough time for him to get sick if she had a contagious disease. The only thing that worked that fast was…ugh, food poisoning.

"Not a germ, Leona. Eli thinks"—she lowered her voice—"Eli thinks she might have been poisoned."

"He told you that?!" Eli was usually pretty closemouthed about his cases. He didn't have many cases this serious, though, so sometimes a detail slipped out here and there. Enough that Ruth and I could put things together.

"He didn't say no when I asked."

I hated to admit it, but I wasn't too upset by the news that Amelia might have been poisoned. It was good news for my eggs, anyway. "Great!" I said, before I realized how callous that sounded.

"Not great. There are Scramblers everywhere downtown, still desperate to find the golden egg and pretty ticked off that they haven't cracked the riddle yet. Margie Morrow is trying to do damage control by hollering into the microphone, but nobody is listening to her. Plus, once Aaron got sick, a group of people ganged up on Sara, convinced that she poisoned Amelia, and she had to close the café for the rest of the day just so they'd stop harassing her. It's total chaos."

My heart sank. Who cared if my eggs had a good reputation if my one loyal customer had to close her café? If the town sentiment was against Sara, it was very possible that nobody would eat Easter brunch—or any meal ever again—at the Rx Café. I couldn't just sit around and watch her business fail.

"We have to do something," I said. "If people don't eat Sara's food tomorrow, she won't be able to recover. She might have to close."

Ruth sighed. "What can we possibly do, though? Go around and convince every single person in town that she had nothing to do with it?"

A smile spread slowly across my face. "That's exactly what we're going to do. Tomorrow morning, you and I are going to Easter service at the Church of the Everlasting to give our condolences to Pastor Cal...and while we're there, we're going to evangelize for the Rx Café. Everyone's going to be there, right? It's the perfect opportunity to set things straight."

Ruth was quiet for a minute, and then a loud laugh erupted from the phone.

"What's so funny?" I asked.

"I'm just picturing everybody's faces when the two of us walk through the church door and sit down on a pew. You in your dirty overalls and me with a crystal in my cleavage. They all might keel over like Amelia did."

"Too soon," I said, swallowing the lump that rose in my throat at the mention of her name. "I'm not ready to laugh about that yet."

"We've gotta laugh or we've gotta cry," Ruth said, her voice sympathetic. "Speaking of gotta, I gotta go get my client brushed out. I'll see you tomorrow when the church bells ring."

"When the church bells ring," I echoed.

Chapter 5

Easter Sunday, Day 2

R uth and I sat near the back of the church. Surprisingly, I felt right at home. The Church of the Everlasting had a small sanctuary, with a simple peaked roof and spare, rustic décor, almost as if it were a farmhouse rather than a place of worship. I could hardly see the pulpit through the pastel rainbow of beautifully decorated hats in front of us, though. The women of Honeytree had gone all out, whether out of respect for Amelia or because of Easter tradition, I couldn't say.

Though I wasn't wearing a hat, I'd done my best getting dressed using pieces from my old life as a Beverly Hills housewife—pieces that I'd crammed in the depths of my closet when I moved back to Honeytree, thinking I wouldn't need them on the farm. I wore a cashmere twin set, a diamond tennis bracelet that my ex-husband, Peterson, gave me for our first Valentine's Day as a married couple, a tweed pencil skirt that hugged my rear end a little tighter than I remembered, and nude pumps even though I'd sworn I'd never wear heels again. Speaking of swearing, if I hadn't been sitting in church,

I'd have been swearing over how those shoes pinched my toes.

"How do people stand wearing these every day? How did *I* stand wearing them?" I whispered to Ruth. Ruth had done her best to look presentable, too. She'd wrestled her usually wild mane of hair into a French twist. A few tendrils escaped and framed her face, drawing attention to her dark blue eyes. The navy dress she wore complemented them perfectly, even though it was a little sedate compared to her usual rainbow fantasy wardrobe. At least she was still carrying her huge purple tapestry purse, otherwise I might not recognize her.

"Pain is all relative," she said. "Those shoes didn't feel so bad when something else hurt worse."

"Isn't that the truth," I said, pushing down the memories of my old life that rushed to the surface at her words. I was lucky to have a friend as compassionate and wise as Ruth. I scooted my feet out of the shoes so my toes would stop screaming and nodded up to the front. "Maybe you should be the one up there giving the sermon instead of Pastor Cal."

The woman sitting on the pew in front of me turned around. "I can't believe he's up to preaching today, after you-know-what."

"It's such a tragedy," Ruth said, nodding. "Poor Cal."

"Poor Amelia, you mean," the woman said. "Her life was nothing but serving others, and then cut short like that?" She *tsk*ed and then, seeing Preston stand and walk across the dais to the pulpit, turned back to face the front, leaning forward as she anticipated what he was going to say.

Preston adjusted the microphone and cleared his throat. The whole sanctuary seemed to hold its breath, waiting for him to start. He grimaced, shaking his head slightly as he began. "I know you're hoping to see Pastor Goodbody up here, not me.

Regrettably, Cal is unable to deliver his Easter sermon today."

The crowd gave a collective sigh and sat back in their seats. Apparently Honeytree was hungry for a glimpse of the grieving widower. Murmurs rippled up and down the pews.

"I know, I know." Preston held up his hands defensively. "I'm disappointed, too. He'll be at the reception after the service, though, and you can express your condolences at that time." He went on to introduce the substitute pastor from Roseburg, an elderly gentleman with a large mustache, who proceeded to deliver a dry and droning sermon. I'm embarrassed to admit that I was too busy planning out my arguments to convince people to eat brunch at the Rx after the service to actually listen.

I tested out my first strategy in the receiving line for Pastor Cal. "That service sure worked up an appetite," I commented to the substitute pastor, who happened to be in line ahead of me.

He nodded politely. "I hear they have cookies and juice over by the piano."

"I'm going to the Rx after this. They have some fantastic brunch specials," I smiled brightly. "Sara makes great pancakes."

His face purpled and his mustache quivered slightly. His mouth worked as he formulated his reply. "Stay away from there. That Jezebel killed Mrs. Goodbody sure as I'm standing here."

I blinked. "Are you talking about Sara?"

"I don't know her name. All I know is she's got the devil's marks all over her."

He meant Sara's tattoos, I was pretty sure. Heat rose from my chest up to my cheeks and sweat started pouring from my underarms. I took off my cashmere cardigan and flapped my arms a little to dry them out. "Don't be silly," I said. "What would Sara have against Amelia?"

"Who's to say. But all evil will come to light," he muttered. He shuffled forward as the line moved toward Pastor Cal.

Well, that was a disaster. When I reached the front of the line where a life-size color portrait of Amelia was displayed on a white easel, I was shocked. Pastor Cal stood beside her photo looking like a different man. Yesterday, he appeared young, vibrant, and ready to take on the world. Today, his face looked puffy, lined, and fifteen years older. Preston stood next to him and seemed to be propping him up.

"I'm so very sorry about Amelia," I said, grasping Cal's hand. I hoped that he wouldn't recognize me as the person who found her body, but I needn't have worried. He looked right through me. I doubt he even registered my words, let alone my face.

"Thank you for your thoughts," he said tonelessly, withdrawing his hand from mine and extending it to Ruth in line behind me.

"Should he be here?" I asked Preston under my breath as I shook his hand, too. "It seems like he might need more time to grieve—private time."

"He insisted," Preston murmured. "Anyway, Amelia would have wanted him to stay in the public eye. The election is so close, and the campaign was dear to her heart."

Of course. The election. But even if he pulled off a win over Margie Morrow, how could Cal possibly lead the town if he was devastated with grief?

"Look out for him, OK? Tell him to slow down if he needs to. We'll all understand," Ruth added worriedly, sharing a look with me. It was clear she agreed with my assessment. Pastor

40

Cal was in no shape for public appearances.

We headed for the refreshments table. Even if I was planning to make a show of eating the Rx Café's Easter brunch, that didn't mean I couldn't grab a couple of purse cookies. As Ruth and I perused the selections—snickerdoodles and rocky road cookies donated in Amelia's memory by the Pastry Palace, a small, handwritten sign informed us—the tail end of a conversation caught my ear.

"She was sick as soon as she ate her eggs. I saw her swallow and then make a dash for the bathroom." I recognized the voice. It was flowered raincoat lady, Tammy. "And *then* Aaron, you know, Jennifer's boy? He did CPR on her, and *he* immediately got sick. The food poisoning must have transferred from her mouth to his."

I turned with a cookie in each hand and saw Tammy surrounded by a gaggle of fascinated onlookers, the feathers on their Easter bonnets bobbing as they hung on her every word.

"It wasn't immediately, Tammy!" I blurted out.

The group turned to stare, and I felt Ruth tense beside me.

"Pardon?" Tammy said, adjusting her yellow hat. It perfectly matched the yellow flowers on her ruffled maxi-dress. "I don't follow."

"Aaron didn't get sick immediately. I watched him do CPR on Amelia at nine a.m., but he didn't get sick until late in the afternoon."

Tammy sucked in her cheeks. "So? I don't see what that has to do with anything." She abruptly turned back to the group and they huddled together like football players before a big play.

I tucked the cookies in my purse so they wouldn't crumble

and bulldozed between Tammy and the woman next to her. "*So* that means Amelia's breakfast was fine. She wasn't poisoned at the Rx Café."

Tammy barked a laugh. "Don't tell me what I saw! I was there—she ate those eggs, and then she was sicker than a dog. You can't argue with simple cause and effect."

"Well, you came to church and then spread falsehoods about a dead woman just to get attention. Was it the sermon that caused that?" I held my cardigan over my arm like a shield and braced myself for church-lady attack. The tight group loosened and several people took a step back, eyeing me with new wariness. Great. Why couldn't I keep my mouth shut? I was here to restore the Rx's reputation, not destroy my own.

I tried desperately to get back on track. "All I'm saying is that if it took six hours for Aaron to get sick, then it must have a while for Amelia, too. It wasn't her breakfast that poisoned her."

Tammy turned the color of a boiled beet underneath her spray tan. I thought she might explode right there in the reception hall. "Of course you'd say that. They were your eggs she ate, weren't they?" She looked around at her audience and their gaping mouths and grinned triumphantly. She pointed an accusing finger at me. "Leona Davis, you keep your poison eggs and your poison opinions to your own self! Honeytree doesn't need any more of either of them!"

I felt a tug on my elbow. Ruth.

"Come on," she urged. "You aren't winning any friends here."

One glance around the hall and it was clear she was right. Daggers were coming at me from all corners. At this rate I was doing more damage than repair—to my own business and maybe to the Rx's, too. Plus, I was making the scene at what amounted to a memorial for Amelia, and that was poor behavior on my part.

"Sorry," I mouthed over my shoulder at Preston, who was doing his best to move the receiving line along and get Cal out of there as quickly as possible. He smiled tightly at me, ever the diplomat.

Outside on the church steps, Ruth's face was still and serious. "I don't think you could have picked a worse person to tick off than Tammy Jenson. That woman has a viper's tongue and an elephant's memory. Seriously, Leona. Why'd you have to butt in on her conversation?"

"Did you hear what she was saying? It was a complete fiction! You're the one who always says that you shouldn't spread gossip unless it's true," I sputtered. Ruth's salon chair might be known countywide as the place to get the skinny on any local rumors, but she was scrupulous about verifying her facts. Surely she'd understand why I needed to correct Tammy's version of the story.

"She's always got a bug up her butt and a tale to tell, and everyone knows that next week it'll be something new. Nobody pays her any mind…it's when *she* pays *you* mind that you need to start worrying."

"They were eating it up. I saw their faces."

"Think of it this way," Ruth said over her shoulder as she headed down the steps toward the street. "Tammy's like those tabloids at the grocery store. You read the headlines while you stand in line, right? You giggle over them to pass the time. But you don't buy them and take them home. Those folks were just rubbernecking for entertainment purposes. But once you piped up? Now people are paying attention. Now you're that celebrity who's like, 'No, I did *not* fornicate with aliens!' Your

43

ears prick up, right? Like maybe he *did*, when you thought it was just silliness before."

I hoped she was wrong. I caught up to her and matched her stride as we ambled down the hill. "Where are we going?"

Ruth grinned at me. "We're going to have Easter brunch."

Chapter 6

The first thing I noticed when we walked in the front door of the Rx Café was that Sara had added ivory tablecloths and fresh flowers to the tables. The silverware and water goblets gleamed in the flicker of the tealight candle at each place setting. The second thing I noticed was that not a soul was seated in the restaurant.

Sara paced worriedly behind the counter, rubbing her hands together and cracking her knuckles. "I'm so glad you're here!" she blurted out when she saw us. "I didn't think anybody was going to come."

"Church just let out," Ruth said soothingly. "I'm sure people will trickle down once they pay their respects to Cal Goodbody."

Sara moaned at the mention of Cal's name. "I'm pretty sure they won't. If they're Pastor Cal's supporters, they've already decided I'm the devil who killed his wife. Why is this happening to me?" She ran her hands through her short hair. "Ugh, what am I doing? You're standing here hungry and I'm just whining. Come on, you get the best seat in the house." She led us toward a table near the center of the café, but Ruth shook her head.

"We're sitting right in the front window where everyone can

see. We want people to know that we aren't afraid to eat here."

Sara's chin crumpled and she blinked rapidly, sniffing as she turned on her heel and took us to the table Ruth requested. She put the special, hand-drawn brunch menus down in front of us and offered us a wobbly smile. "Thank you for believing me. Really."

I put my pale, freckled hand on top of her olive, tattooed one and patted it in what I hoped was a comforting way. "Of course we do. It's pretty clear that whatever killed Amelia was something she ate hours before breakfast. If anyone poisoned her, they did it on Friday night, not Saturday morning."

Sara's elfin face paled slightly, and she took a step back from our table, shaking her head. "Oh, please don't say that! Don't tell anyone that—it'll just make things worse!"

Ruth gaped at her. "What do you mean, hon?"

But before Sara could explain, the front door opened and Margie Morrow swept in, patting her helmet hairdo importantly. Doc Morrow, an unassuming man with a shockingly bad combover that did nothing to conceal his very bald head, carried her handbag and shuffled two steps behind.

"We're here for brunch!" Margie announced. Her husband, who owned and operated the pharmacy connected to the café and was Sara's landlord, scooted around Margie and hung her purse on the back of a chair. She sniffed and pointed to a different chair and he quickly moved it. "That's better."

Sara looked strangely relieved. "I'll get your menus and be right with you!" She darted back to the kitchen and then bustled around filling the Morrows' water goblets. She filled ours, too, but as quickly and with as little eye contact as possible. She almost seemed afraid of us.

"Weird," I said, following Sara's frantic movements around

the café. I lowered my voice so it was barely audible and leaned toward Ruth. "Why do you think Sara asked us not to tell anybody? Wouldn't that remove any suspicion that her breakfast was to blame for Amelia's death?"

"You'd think so."

Sara darted a glance at us and then, when she saw our eyes on her, scurried into the kitchen area. Strange behavior for an innocent woman. Maybe I'd been too quick to defend Sara from her detractors. She was definitely hiding something, and I was going to find out what. I sipped my ice-cold water as I waited for her to come back to take our order.

A knock came at the window and I inhaled the sip of ice water in my mouth and almost fell out of my chair. Ruth cracked up at my expression. Once I finished coughing, I turned and saw the culprit—Eli was grinning at me from outside. Before I could stop her, Ruth motioned for him to join us.

He sauntered in, clearly way too pleased at the reaction he'd elicited. He grabbed a chair and pulled it up to our table, scooting the flowers and candles out of his way so he could put his elbows on the table. "I saw you in here like an animal in the zoo and I couldn't resist tapping on the glass," he said. The corners of his eyes crinkled, and if he wasn't so cute, I would have kicked him under the table.

"Are you trying to kill me?" I asked him. "You know I hate being surprised."

Eli put his hand over his heart. "On my honor, I am only here to serve and protect."

"Oh, Sheriff Ramiiirez!" Margie trilled from her table. "So good to see you out and about in the commuuunity!"

Eli rolled his eyes and turned around slightly to answer her. "That's my job, ma'am."

Margie nudged her husband who was slouched down in his chair and seemed to be falling asleep. "Invite him to golf, honey."

Doc made a face. "I don't really like golf, Marge. I keep telling you that."

"Pish!" Margie said gaily, waving her hand. "He doesn't mean that. He loves golfing, especially with important people. Like you." She beamed at Eli, who turned back around and rolled his eyes again for our benefit.

Sara emerged from the kitchen with her order pad and stopped short when she caught sight of Eli sitting with us. She took a deep breath, blew it out, and headed for our table. "Are you joining the ladies, Sheriff?" she asked politely. She shook her head slightly "no" as though hoping for that answer.

"Yes, he is!" Ruth said firmly. "My treat."

"It's always a treat to eat with you, Ruth." Eli winked at her and Ruth flushed happily. He was such a shameless flirt. It did make him fun to have around, even if it caused me the teensiest bit of jealousy when he gave his attention to other women. I didn't have a claim on him, though—and I didn't want anyone to have a claim on *me*—so I tried not to let it bother me.

"Great. Just great," Sara said through slightly clenched teeth. "What'll you have?"

Eli leaned so he could see my menu, his well-muscled bicep pressing against my shoulder. I have to say, I didn't mind a bit. I could admire the merchandise even if I didn't want to purchase, right? We placed our orders with Sara, and she left us and went to the Morrows to get theirs next. Eli nudged my foot playfully under the table and I elbowed him.

"Do we *have* to order off the special menu?" Margie trumpeted. Her husband sank lower in his seat. "Can I get something else?"

"Sure. Well, I mean…if I have it in the back," Sara mumbled, darting a guilty look at me. Obviously, she didn't have eggs, since she'd refused my order. I crossed my fingers under the table and hoped Margie ordered an omelet.

Margie rubbed her hands together greedily. "Do you have any more of those itty-bitty smoked salmon thingybobs you made for the cocktail party? I want a whole plate. Amelia hogged all of 'em on Friday and I only got one."

Sara's hand holding her order pad trembled slightly as she gave a panicked glance at Eli's back. I froze in my seat. This is what she'd been worried about earlier. Amelia didn't just eat Sara's food for breakfast on Saturday—she'd eaten it Friday night, too.

"What party?" I asked. I thought I knew everything going on in this town. "I didn't hear about a party."

"Sure you did," Margie simpered. "It was the Chamber of Commerce meet-and-greet for the mayoral candidates. Everyone was there."

"Not everybody. I wasn't," I said. "Ruth wasn't, either."

Ruth cleared her throat, a small, dry, polite sound. I stared at her. Small, dry, and polite were not things that Ruth Chapman was—ever.

"Actually, I *was* there." She gave me an apologetic shrug. "What? I have two businesses in town! Of course I'm a member of the Chamber of Commerce."

I frowned at her in surprise. "Why didn't you invite me? I'm always your plus-one."

"You hate parties."

"No, I don't!"

"You hate *this* kind of party. Anyway, it was only for

constituents. You live out of town, so you can't vote in the election." Ruth winced apologetically, and the room fell into awkward silence. Sara took the opportunity to flee for the kitchen.

"Why didn't you say anything about the party when we were discussing what Amelia ate last night?" My voice came out a little louder than I intended it to, but I was pretty ticked off. She'd clearly been avoiding the topic or it would have come up naturally—there was something about it she didn't want me to know.

She shrugged, avoiding my eyes.

I squinted at her. "Who *was* your plus-one?"

Eli butted in. "I was. Why are we talking about Amelia Goodbody's dinner?"

I rolled my eyes at him. "That's when she was poisoned, obviously. Try and keep up!"

Margie Morrow gasped and put a hand to her chest. I thought for a second she might throw her head back and pretend to faint like in a bad movie. "You don't think someone tried to kill her at the Chamber of Commerce cocktail party?!"

"Of course not," Eli said firmly. "I know what happened to Amelia. The official medical examiner's report will be released tomorrow, but I can say that her death will be ruled an accident."

Margie let out a dramatic sigh of relief. "Thank heavens. I wouldn't want to think that anyone in Honeytree would do something so…so…*reprehensible.* Am I right, Warren?" She poked her husband in the arm and he jerked his head up. Had he really been sleeping through all this?

Doc wiped a bit of drool from the corner of his mouth. "Yes, dear, quite right."

Margie clasped her hands. "Wonderful. Then I hope nobody will argue if I order a round of mimosas."

Nobody argued.

That is, until we left the restaurant.

Then we all turned on each other.

"Don't give me a guilt trip, Leona." Ruth glared at me as we stood on the sidewalk in front of her shop.

"I'm not!"

"I see that sour expression. You're mad about sitting home alone on Friday night. But don't tell me you wouldn't have turned me down if I'd asked you, anyway! You'd have said, 'I'm not attending any party where I have to wear hose.'"

Eli turned to me. "Are you upset Ruth invited me?" he asked, butting in as usual.

I made a face at him. "Actually, you're the one I'm mad at, not Ruth."

"Me?!" His eyebrows shot up. "What'd I do?"

I tapped my foot, waiting for him to figure it out. But of course, he didn't. *Men.* "How in the world can you say that Amelia's death was an accident when Aaron Alpin was poisoned six hours after he gave her CPR? That's preposterous."

He shifted uncomfortably. "You know I can't discuss details of a pending investigation. You can get a copy of the report tomorrow from the county if you call, though."

I rolled my eyes. "You can be sure I will. I can't help wondering how Amelia was *accidentally* poisoned."

And as I looked between my two best friends, I couldn't help wondering what else they were keeping from me.

Chapter 7

Monday, Day 3

The next morning was dark and drizzly. Boots, my crooked-toed house chicken, perched on the arm of my chair as I finished my coffee, peering hopefully at my breakfast muffin. I'd given up on trying to get her to sleep in the coop with the rest of the flock. Now she nested in an old dresser drawer near my bed at night and followed me around the house and yard during the day, chattering and clucking as I did my house and yard work. She'd even sit on my lap in the evening while I watched TV or read. It turned out that she was pretty good company, especially once I figured out how to rig her with a calico diaper that kept the hm-hm off the upholstery.

I plucked a blueberry out of the remaining half of my muffin and gave it to her. She snatched it and flapped down to the floor, trilling and gloating over her prize. I crammed the rest of my muffin down the hatch, slugged my coffee, and pulled on my muck boots over my sweatpants just as my phone alarm pinged. *Time for chores.*

I had a daily routine on the farm that I executed with

precision. Routines made things easy because I never had to think about whether I'd done a task. I didn't have to decide whether to do something—I just did it. Did I put out the oyster shell crumbles so the layers would have enough calcium? Yep. Did I refill the waterers? Yep, whether they needed it or not. Did I collect the eggs? Yep, twice a day, every day.

I put up my hood against the miserable weather and headed outside. Boots followed me down the steps but changed her mind when she felt the first few drops of rain. She retreated to the porch, squawking at me from her roost on the railing that I was making a terrible mistake.

"Don't worry, I'm not a turkey!" I called to her over my shoulder. I'd heard from old timers that some breeds of turkeys were so dumb, they'd look up at falling rain until they drowned. That probably wasn't true, but it seemed like the kind of rumor chickens would believe.

The rest of my birds were perfectly content to be out in the weather. All eighty-something of them were out in the enormous fenced run, anticipating my arrival—and all eighty-something looked pretty soggy and bedraggled with their wet feathers clinging to them. Phyllis and Cher, my two Polish hens, looked like they could hardly see; their feathered topknots were plastered over their faces. Maybe Boots was right to stay on the porch.

I filled the feeders, much to the flock's ever-clucking delight, and threw out some scratch to keep them busy. I buzzed through the rest of the chores until I reached the last task. My favorite, collecting the eggs. I hummed as I filled two wire baskets with the morning's haul and then gingerly carried the baskets around to the back porch to wash, sort, and store in the egg fridge. I filled up a full 30-egg flat with pullet-size eggs and another half full of eggs that were approaching regular size.

My babies were growing up. Sniff.

Boots came around to investigate and I shooed her away before she got too curious and pecked an egg. I fed my chickens plenty of protein to ensure they didn't turn into egg-eaters, but that was a habit that was hard to break once it got started. "Go lay your own," I admonished her.

She scratched at the porch floorboards and pretended to eat something, then fixed me with one beady eye.

"Go on," I said, nudging her with my boot. She hopped over into a potted plant and snuggled into the leaves. Sometimes I swore she could understand me—and sometimes I swore I really was turning into a crazy chicken lady. There were worse fates, I chuckled to myself as I scooped up the flats of sorted eggs and took them to the porch fridge. I swung the door open and was dismayed by what I saw—the fridge was completely packed. There was no way I could fit even a single flat inside.

"Shoot," I muttered. I'd have to store them in my kitchen fridge for now, at least until I could unload some of these eggs. In another era, I'd have just stored them in boxes on the porch—unwashed eggs could keep for weeks, if not months, at cool spring temperatures. But state guidelines said I had to wash and refrigerate, and I wasn't going to jeopardize my business.

I took them inside and cleared out the middle shelf of the fridge so the large flats would fit. And they barely fit. This afternoon's collection would double the number of eggs. And tomorrow's eggs would quadruple them. There was no way I could fit that many eggs in my fridge even if I took all my regular food out. I had to find somewhere to sell them or they'd go to waste.

I poured another cup of coffee and called Sara. She answered with a cheerful, "Rx Café, we're good for what ails you."

"How many eggs do you think you'll need this week?" I asked.

"Oh, hi Leona." Her voice was suddenly hesitant. "I'm afraid I won't need any."

"Even if you don't have eggs on the menu, pancakes and waffles use a lot of eggs," I protested, panic sliding up my throat. "You didn't order more from the grocery store, did you?"

"Nobody's coming in, even for pancakes. I decided to just close this week." Sara lowered her voice. "This Goodbody stuff is all anyone is talking about. People don't feel safe eating here. They're worried about getting salmonella and keeling over like Amelia did."

"But she didn't have—"

"I know."

"And factory farms are worse than—"

"I know." Sara sounded genuinely sympathetic. "It's just going to take a few days to get sorted out. Hang onto my order. I figure by next week, everyone's going to be dying for an egg breakfast and I can re-open. *Ugh*, that came out wrong."

"I'll say," I said wryly. "Let's not have anyone else dying for eggs around here."

"No kidding."

We hung up, and I fortified myself with a few more sips of coffee before I dialed the Greasy Spoon. I held my breath while I waited for the line to answer.

"It's a great day at the Greasy Spoon. This is Jillian. What can I help you with?"

"Hi, this is Leona from Lucky Cluck Farm. Just checking to see if Ed needs any eggs this week?"

"Let me ask." She put me on hold and returned a few moments later. "Doesn't look like it. People are being very picky about where their eggs come from. Sorry about that."

"I'm offering them at half price due to a surplus," I said desperately.

"Maybe next week? Try back then." Jillian hung up the phone.

I let out a sigh and bumped my fist gently against the kitchen tabletop. This whole thing was stupid. If only Amelia had eaten breakfast at home before the Easter Scramble. Then people would be blaming her death on kale smoothies or whatever she ate. Not that I'd wish this on kale farmers, either.

But that's the thing—people weren't blaming it on eggs in general, were they? They were blaming it on *my* eggs. Sure, they might forget I was the egg supplier eventually, but I couldn't afford to wait for that. It might take years. There was only one way to sort this out, and it was to show that salmonella poisoning had nothing to do with Amelia's death. And that meant I needed to see what *actually* killed her.

The county coroner's office phone was answered by a nasal woman with a brisk, businesslike clip to her voice. "Yes?"

"I'd like to get a copy of Amelia Goodbody's autopsy report," I said sweetly.

"Mhm." Clicking keys. "Fax or mail?"

"Fax, please." I gave the fax number for Ruth's salon.

Clickety-click. "And how are you related to the deceased?"

"Uh…" I paused, debating whether to mention the truth—*I'm the one who found her body*—or offer some sanitized version. "Concerned citizen?"

The clicking stopped. Bad sign. "I can't issue you a copy at this time."

"Isn't the report considered public information?!"

"Mhm. But we can't send you the report unless you're a family member or involved in the case."

I groaned internally. I was going to have to go there. "I'm involved. I found her body. And she—well, she ate something that was produced by my farm."

A pause. More clicking. "Have you been charged with a crime?"

"No—not yet," I added, hoping that the mere possibility would gain me some traction.

She sniffed. "You can review a redacted copy at your local sheriff's office, ma'am. Have a good day." A final, decisive click, and the line went dead.

Now I had to put on real pants and go to town. Mother-clucker.

I located some mostly clean jeans and a flannel shirt and then wrestled my mane of blonde-and-gray curls into a bun and stabbed it with a few bobby pins to keep it that way. If the rebellion of freckles across my face didn't give me away, I almost looked civilized. Certainly cleaned up enough to pass as a regular person who just wanted to know regular stuff like how a nice dead lady bit the dust.

"No, you cannot go with me," I said to Boots, who was waiting for me on the doormat, having laid her egg in the pansies. I put her egg in the fridge and left her locked in the bathroom with a mayonnaise lid full of mealworms to keep her out of trouble while I was gone. Well, she'd probably find trouble, but hopefully not too much.

In town, I parked my Suburban across from the Do or Dye, right in front of the sheriff's office. Eli's grinning face greeted me as soon as I pushed through the gilt-lettered door. Shoot.

57

So much for flying under the radar. Eli's radar always honed right in on me.

"I knew you'd be in here today," he said, chuckling and shaking his head.

"How'd you know when I only just decided?" I asked tartly. When he wisely didn't answer, I added, "Well, if you know why I'm here, then you know what I want."

He slid a blue binder across the desk, and I sat down across from him to flip through it. The pages of the report were in individual plastic sleeves, and certain personal information like surname and address had been blacked out with permanent marker to protect Amelia's privacy—like we didn't know all that stuff anyway.

I quickly scanned the pages. As Eli had hinted at yesterday, her death had been ruled an accident, but the cause of death was "poisoning by tetrodotoxin." I let out a sigh of relief. Not salmonella. Not *E. coli*. Not listeria. Nothing that I'd ever heard of in relation to food poisoning or chickens or eggs.

But then—what *had* poisoned her? I pointed to the word. "What is this, anyway?"

Eli came around the desk and looked over my shoulder. "Oh, yeah. I asked the medical examiner the same thing. Apparently, it's a really toxic poison that some animals make naturally, including the newts that live in the creek where Amelia was found. They think she probably fell into the water while she was hiding the egg and somehow got one in her mouth."

I stared at him. "She died of accidentally swallowing a newt?"

He shrugged. "Seems that way."

"That's the dumbest thing I've ever heard." I snapped the binder closed. "Don't tell me you buy that."

His brow furrowed as he studied my face. "I take it you

don't."

I shook my head. He pulled a chair over so it faced me and took a seat, scooting forward until our knees almost touched. "Why not? What did you see that a highly trained medical examiner missed?"

I made a face. "Now you're making fun of me."

Eli shook his head. "No, I can tell you have a good reason for thinking that—you always have a good reason to back up what you say. So I'm genuinely interested to hear."

My cheeks flushed slightly at the compliment. Ruth would say Eli was just currying favor, but she was as susceptible to his compliments as anybody. Apparently, he'd given her enough compliments that she invited him to be her plus-one instead of me!

Not to say I was jealous. I wasn't.

OK, maybe a little. But I wasn't jealous of Ruth—I was jealous of Eli. Ruth was *my* best friend, not his!

Anyway, I never knew him to be a liar. A flirt, maybe, but he didn't try to trick people, so he probably did want to hear my opinion. I thought back to Amelia's body stretched out behind the bush on the creekbank. "Amelia's dress was dry when I found her. There's no way she fell into the water before she died."

Eli licked his lower lip absentmindedly, considering the information. "Newts spend part of their life cycle on land. Maybe she slipped in the mud and accidentally swallowed one that was hibernating in the leaf litter."

"Really?" I stared at him. "Really? She slipped and landed mouth-down on a newt? That's your theory?"

He spread his hands and shrugged. "That's the best I've got. The ME says there's no suggestion of foul play. It's called accidental death for a reason. Weird accidents happen all the time. One time I got called to a car wreck that happened because a seagull got skewered on a car antenna. I mean, what are the chances of that?"

"A lot higher than the chances of Amelia Goodbody laying on her back in a clean, dry dress after having slipped and fallen face-first on a newt." I crossed my arms triumphantly. "Anyway, it took Aaron Alpin six hours to develop symptoms after he did CPR. Why did it kill her instantly, but not him? How's he doing, by the way?"

"He pulled through, but he'll be in the hospital for a few more days," Eli said absentmindedly, running his hands through his dark, silver-shot hair. It was the same unconscious gesture he'd always used even back in high school when we were a couple. I didn't mind one bit that he still wore his hair the same way, short on the sides and a little longer on top so sometimes a wavy lock escaped and hung down on his forehead, like right now. I resisted the urge to smooth it back into place. One didn't fix the chief deputy's hair while he was on duty.

"That's good. Now tell me, if there was a newt in her mouth, how come he didn't just immediately kick the bucket, too?"

Eli took a deep breath and let it out slowly. "You're right. Shoot."

I nodded smugly. "She got that poison in her system a whole lot earlier than Saturday morning. And it wasn't from a stupid newt."

He stood up abruptly and left the room through a depressing gray metal door that matched the rest of the depressing gray décor, returning a moment later with his sheriff's jacket. "Come on, let's go."

I pushed back my chair and stood up. "Where are we going?"

"We're going to pay a visit to an expert."

Chapter 8

I tagged after Eli as he strode briskly down the street. At first, I thought he was heading for the Rx Café, but to my surprise, he turned into the pharmacy next door instead. The small building had large plate-glass windows that showcased a collection of dusty giftware—teacups, music boxes, windchimes, and poseable harlequin dolls that had been collectible thirty years ago. In the back of the store, compact shelves were stocked with all the necessities of life: Tampax, Alka-Seltzer, cough drops, and Tylenol.

A hand-lettered sign taped in the window read, "No tree nuts. No peanuts. No wingnuts."

Eli held open the door and I stepped through it onto the unassuming brown carpet, threading my way through the tchotchke displays to the pharmacy window where the top of Doc Morrow's head was visible through the sliding glass. That's who Eli must have meant when he said he was consulting an expert. I supposed a pharmacist would know about things like poisons.

Eli rapped at the glass and Doc looked up, his mouth an "O" of surprise. Before he could slide open the window, Margie appeared pertly from the back room, beaming and adjusting the loud purple scarf she wore around her neck. When she wasn't at City Hall, Margie could often be found here working the register. In a town as small as ours, the mayor's salary barely amounted to minimum wage and the job was only half-time. It made more sense for her to wrap gifts and ring up prescriptions in her husband's store than to pay someone else to do it.

"So sorry. I didn't hear you come in," she chirped at us. "What can I help you with?" Her eyes darted slyly to the display of condoms behind the counter and then back to me and Eli. I felt the heat crawl up my neck and I fanned myself before my flush turned into a flash. I elbowed Eli and he jumped to attention.

"Uh, I need to speak with Doc. Coupla questions about a case."

"Is this about Amelia?" Margie's eyes lit up when Eli nodded. "Ooh, sounds important. I'll get him right away. I'm sure he'll give you *special access*." She turned and rapped at the glass just as Eli had done just moments before, and I rolled my eyes.

"Special access," I mouthed silently to Eli, and he bit his lip to keep from laughing.

Doc slid open the window grudgingly, and I wondered if a person could move any more slowly. He raised his eyebrows with great effort, as though they weighed twenty pounds each. "Yes?"

Margie clung to the window frame as she peered up at her husband. "Warren, the sheriff is investigating Amelia's death and needs *special access*."

Doc frowned in slow motion. "There's no such thing, Marge. I keep telling you that. All my records protected by confidentiality laws." He turned his attention to Eli. "Sorry—unless you have a subpoena, I can't share anything with you."

63

Eli nodded. "This is just a general question, more of a chemistry problem than a medical one."

Doc's face brightened. "Excellent. I love chemistry." He disappeared back into the shelves that held rows of bottled medicines and emerged from a door to the side. He led us to a small dinette table near a sink at the side of the store that seemed out of place amid the merchandise. "Coffee?"

He didn't wait for us to answer, just rinsed two stained coffee cups and poured us each a serving from the pot next to the sink. Then he did the same with a third cup for himself and plunked down at the table. "Welcome to my office," he said magnanimously.

Margie fluttered over and grabbed another coffee cup for herself from the sink. She noisily doctored her cup with a lot of sugar and took a seat, looking annoyed that Doc hadn't poured her coffee along with ours. "OK, I'm ready. You can go ahead," she said, as though Eli were there to talk to her instead of Doc.

Eli cleared his throat. "Well. My question is along these lines: what do you know about tetrodotoxin poisoning?"

Margie gasped and leaned forward, blinking rapidly. "Is that what killed Amelia? I thought it was food poisoning!"

"It wasn't," I said sharply. Then I bit my own tongue. I didn't want to ruin any chance we had at learning what we could from Doc Morrow. I didn't want to alienate Margie, either. She could be a great way to spread the truth about what happened around town, if I could set her straight in a gentler way.

Doc tipped back even further in his chair, his eyes twinkling. "Oh my, I haven't heard that word in some time. Not since pharmacy school, probably. There was a Japanese food craze

64

at the time and our professors were keen to keep us engaged in the classroom. What better way than claiming our sushi takeout could poison us?" He chortled. "You can bet I sat up and listened!"

"I'm not following," Eli said. "What does tetrodotoxin have to do with Japanese food?"

"It doesn't—not much, anyway. It's a toxin produced by pufferfish. Some daring gastrophiles eat pufferfish sushi, but it has to be skillfully prepared or—" Doc made a cutting motion across his neck. "You're a goner. Of course, the fish is quite expensive and hard to find, so none of us needed to worry about a chef slipping any into our California rolls!"

Margie's eyes grew round. "Maybe Amelia should have worried about her sushi."

Eli gave Margie a reassuring smile. "Honeytree doesn't have any Japanese restaurants, and last time I checked, the Rx doesn't serve pufferfish either."

Her voice went up an octave. "But she *did* eat her share of smoked salmon at the cocktail mixer! Everyone's share, actually. Maybe that's what did it!"

Doc rolled his eyes. "Oh, stop. Salmon doesn't contain tetrodotoxin."

"It *might.* And I had some yesterday at Easter brunch!" Red spots bloomed on Margie's cheeks and she began breathing heavily. "Oh my word. I'm feeling a bit queasy." She clapped a hand over her mouth and made a dash for the back room.

I rose to my feet and stared worriedly after her, wondering if I should call the ambulance or go check on her, but Doc motioned for me to sit down.

"She's fine. She's fine. She gets herself worked up over everything. If she'd eaten poisonous pufferfish for brunch

65

yesterday, she'd be dead by now. It's more likely she's been sipping Schnapps in the back room."

"That brings me to my next question," Eli said thoughtfully. "How quickly does the poison work?"

"Varies quite a bit," Doc said, leaning forward so all four legs of the chair were on the floor again. He drained his coffee cup and leaned sideways to set it in the sink nearby. "Could be a half-hour, could be hours. Depends on the person, the dose, the fish itself. But I'll tell you what. A dose high enough to kill you would kick in pretty quickly. We're talking symptoms within thirty minutes. And someone who got a smaller dose would be feeling it in three, four hours. A little shortness of breath, a little numbness. Upset stomach and so forth."

Eli's shoulders relaxed, and he extended a hand to Doc. "Thank you very much, sir. You've been very helpful."

"Right-o. I should get back to pills and bills." Doc pushed himself back from the table and ambled off toward the pharmacist's booth.

"Can you let it go now?" Eli asked when Doc was out of earshot. "The ME's theory is right—the timing works for Amelia accidentally ingesting poison at the creek, then Aaron getting a smaller, sublethal dose from performing CPR. It all fits together."

I shook my head slowly. "It doesn't, though. Not quite. Her dress was clean and dry, so I know she didn't fall in the water or the mud. And the golden egg was still in her hand. She hadn't been there on the creek bank for more than a few minutes before she died, because she didn't have time to hide the egg."

Eli's head jerked toward me in surprise. "How do you know that? We didn't find any egg!"

Oops. When I was giving my official statement, I *might* have left out the part of the story where I found the grand prize egg in Amelia's hand.

"I meant to tell you," I said lamely. "I have it." It was somewhere on my bathroom floor—or maybe in the hamper. I left that part out, too.

Eli wasn't in sheriff mode anymore—he was just plain annoyed. He put his hands on his hips and shook his head disbelievingly. "Why didn't you turn it in?!"

"I don't know. It didn't seem…right? To claim a grand prize right after I found it with a dead person." I squeezed my eyes shut and braced myself for his reply.

"That's because it's not. Obviously, you knew that. If you find a treasure in the hands of a dead woman, that's *evidence*. You *leave it alone*. You don't stick it in your pocket." Eli swore under his breath. "Do you realize what a scandal it's going to be if this comes out? Rumors are already flying about your eggs giving Amelia food poisoning, but of course nobody thinks you did that on purpose. But if you turn in the golden egg and claim a thousand-dollar prize, now you have a motive. Now it looks like more than a tragic accident."

My heart sank and my stomach squeezed, and suddenly I was worried that I might need to follow Margie into the back room in search of a bucket to chuck in. I steadied myself on the table and took a few deep breaths while Eli steamed, still shaking his head.

"I'll give it back," I said quietly. "I'll go tell Margie about it right now and give it back to the city."

I started for the doorway where Margie had disappeared, but Eli caught my arm. "No, don't. Give it to me. I'll bag and tag it and slip it into the evidence box. It'll look like we recovered it at the scene."

I swallowed. "Isn't that illegal?"

He pressed his lips together and gave one swift nod. "But it isn't wrong. I'd rather be in the business of justice than law. I just want to set things right. The faster we can get back to normal around here, the better off everyone will be."

The better off I would be, that was for sure. I didn't understand why Eli would risk his career for me, but I wasn't going to stand in his way. I sighed. "I'll bring it to your office this afternoon."

He gave a curt nod and strode toward the door, ducking to avoid the windchimes that hung from the ceiling. He didn't look back. I couldn't help but worry that I'd lost his goodwill once and for all. Maybe this was the last straw for our friendship, even though it might save my farm. I gnawed my lower lip. That's what I wanted, a successful farm. I didn't need Eli to approve of my every decision, right?

Right.

Chapter 9

Before I could gather my wits and get the heck out of there, Margie reappeared from the back room with reddened, mascara-smeared eyes, dabbing her nose with a tissue. "Sorry you had to see that," she croaked. She glanced up at the pharmacy window where Doc was studiously engaged in his work, and then when she was sure he wasn't paying attention, she turned back to me and made a sad face.

"How are you doing?" I asked. Under her smeary makeup, her face was pale. Maybe she really was sick.

"I've been better. How do I look?" Margie jutted her chin toward me as though I was a mirror.

"Fine," I lied. "Nothing a little lipstick won't fix."

She grabbed her beige pocketbook from behind the counter and rummaged in it. She pulled out a compact and a tube of bright pink lipstick and stretched her lips thin to apply a fresh coat. Then she smacked her lips together, snapping the lid of the lipstick closed with a *pop*. "I need to get back to City Hall, but I'm a wobbly mess. I don't know if I can make it down the street."

I caught a whiff of alcohol on her breath. Maybe that was the real reason for her quease, not the suggestion of tainted salmon. "I'm parked over there, and I'm headed out anyway.

69

I'll walk you." While I wasn't particularly interested in palling around with a drunken Margie Morrow, this was the perfect chance for me to put a bug in her ear about spreading the word that my eggs—and the Rx Café—had nothing to do with Amelia's death.

"Well, aren't you a gem!" Margie beamed at me. I held the door open for her and we turned down Main Street together. A half-second later she added, slurring her words slightly, "I really appreciate your support."

"It's no problem," I said absentmindedly, distracted by the sight of Eli's unmistakable figure a couple of blocks ahead. He'd chosen his profession wisely—he really did look great in uniform.

"Oh yeah, he's a keeper," Margie said, stumbling slightly as she followed my gaze. I held out my arm and she leaned on me heavily. "I wouldn't let him out of my sight, either. He and Ruth Chapman have been getting cozy-cozy."

I smiled tightly. "We're all just friends."

"We Honeytree High alums are all friends, aren't we? I hope I can count on all your votes next month," Margie continued without taking a breath. "I swear, this whole business with Amelia has really thrown a wrench in my campaign. Cal's going to get the pity vote, I'm sure of it. I just wish people weren't so blind to his flaws. He and Amelia aren't perfect, you know. But of course I can't say that *now*."

She turned to me, her expression earnest, her eyes searching my face. "Promise me you won't vote for him. He's no good for this town, with or without that so-called wife of his."

I blinked, surprised by the turn the conversation had taken. "I'm not voting in the election. I live outside the city limits, remember?" I said quickly, still puzzled by what she'd said.

Maybe it was just partisan politics that led her to make comments like that, but I couldn't help but feel that she was bursting at the seams to tell me something. "What's so bad about Pastor Cal, anyway? Everyone seems to love him."

Margie stopped in her tracks and nodded, her expression dark. "Exactly. But what do they *really* know?" Her eyes darted down the street to where Eli had been, but he'd disappeared into the building. Then, after ensuring nobody was witness to our conversation, she leaned close to me, blasting me with peach-Schnapps breath, and whispered, "They're from *Idaho*."

I pretended to be shocked. "Not *Idaho*."

Margie nodded meaningfully, her eyes wide. "They haven't been here two years and suddenly it's like they're king and queen of Honeytree. The perfect couple, right? The charming pastor and his pretty wife. But guess what?" She looked over her shoulder again toward the bank to make sure nobody was looking out the window before continuing. "They weren't even *together*."

I blinked again. "What do you mean, they weren't together?"

A smug smile spread across Margie's face. She knew she had me. She took my arm again and resumed walking toward City Hall. "I can't say how I know, but I know that they weren't happily married. They weren't even living together. Their whole relationship was *fake*."

As much as I wanted to laugh at her old-fashioned expression and prudish morals, the accusation she was leveling was serious. If it came out that their marriage was on the rocks, Pastor Cal would certainly lose his reputation—and maybe his job—at the church. And his hopes at being elected mayor were slim-to-none. Honeytree might be able to forgive the Goodbodys for being separated, but I doubted they'd forgive

71

them for lying about it. Margie's smugness annoyed me, though. Why should I believe her, anyway? She had every reason to smear the Goodbodys' reputation.

"They seemed pretty happy to me," I said, sneaking a look at her in my peripheral vision to see if she'd take the bait. "Every time I saw them together, they were all smiles."

"No, they weren't!" Margie said triumphantly. She stopped again and swelled like a pufferfish as she gripped my arm. "Now, don't tell anyone I said this, but they weren't even speaking to each other at the cocktail party on Friday."

I tugged my arm out of her grasp—she was digging in her fingers so hard it was starting to hurt. "Maybe they were too busy schmoozing with the Chamber of Commerce to chat with each other."

"*And* they left separately." Margie raised her eyebrows and pursed her lips, certain this piece of evidence would damn them in my eyes. "I don't know where Amelia's been staying, but it isn't at home with her husband. Maybe she has a new boyfriend, maybe she doesn't—what do I know?"

I confess that my mouth dropped open. No wonder Margie was having a hard time keeping that bit of information to herself. Amelia Goodbody cheating on her husband? I'd believe she was Audrey Hepburn reincarnated before I'd believe that. But I guess people can have deep secrets and a past they'd rather forget about. Someone who met me now, wearing grubby jeans and with callouses on my palms, would never guess that I spent thirty years as a pampered Beverly Hills housewife. And someone who met me then would never have guessed how miserable I really was, because I always put on a perfect smile. Just like Amelia did.

"It didn't come from me," Margie said slyly, watching my

face. I could tell she hoped I'd spread it all over town.

I shook my head. "I'm not going to tell anyone, don't worry."

Disappointment flashed in her eyes. "Well, bless your heart. We shouldn't speak ill of the dead, poor woman."

We were almost at City Hall, and I knew my chance at gaining Margie's support for my egg business was waning, so I nodded in agreement. "At least we know it wasn't something she ate. Eli assured me that her death was just a fluke. A freak accident. One that has nothing to do with her breakfast."

"A fluke," Margie agreed. She stopped with her hand on the door to the city offices. "You know, sometimes accidents happen for a reason."

I blinked. "Why would you say something like that?"

"They show people's true colors. I mean, you see how broken up Cal is over Amelia's death, right?"

I nodded. The man was clearly devastated by her loss.

"Well." Margie looked around us again and stepped out of the way of the door so a city worker could exit, then waited for him to walk down the block before she continued. "I can't blame him for dumping her if she was a liability to his campaign. But I can't respect him for crying over her now that she's gone. That fluke did him a favor—now he should do us the favor of keeping his crocodile tears to himself. I've been in politics a long time now, and nothing turns my stomach like someone capitalizing on a tragedy. It sickens me."

My mind raced. Maybe Margie was right—maybe the Goodbodys weren't so good. A troubled marriage, a messy breakup, all swept under the rug so that Cal Goodbody could get elected mayor. But then again, maybe none of it was true. Maybe Cal and Amelia were as happy as they seemed, and Cal was truly devastated by his wife's death. Margie might be spreading lies to cement her tenure in City Hall.

"Are you feeling all right, hon?"

I nodded. "It's just a lot to take in."

"It is, it is." Margie smiled broadly at me. "But people need to know the truth. It's nice to talk to someone who understands. You're good friends with Ruth Chapman, isn't that right? I know you said you weren't going to tell anyone, but if you need to share with someone, well…I find her to be very understanding, too."

She nodded across the street to Ruth's salon. Through the window, I could see a cluster of women, including the raincoat trio from the library, with their highlighted heads together. Of course, Margie wanted me to tell Ruth what she'd revealed about Amelia and Cal. There was no better way to disseminate information than from Ruth's chair. Her words traveled faster than the weekly newspaper and were more trusted, too. But Margie didn't know one thing—even if I told her the rumor, Ruth would never betray my confidence. Our friendship was too old and deep-rooted for that nonsense.

I nodded politely. "Good luck with your campaign, Margie."

"And good luck with your little egg farm," Margie replied, straightening up. All trace of her alcoholic slur was gone, and her eyes were suddenly focused and clear, making me wonder if she'd ever been drunk to begin with. "It'd be a shame if that didn't work out for you."

Chapter 10

"I can't believe she said that," Ruth declared as she ran a wide-toothed comb through my hair. Somehow she'd convinced me to get one of her special herbal conditioning treatments while I caught her up on my conversation with Marge-in-Charge. "Do you think it was a threat?"

I shrugged and winced as Ruth tugged out a knot in my curls. "I think she was letting me know that she understood my objective in walking with her—to restore Lucky Cluck Farm's reputation. She knew it wasn't out of the goodness of my heart. And maybe she was also letting me know that she was up for a little quid pro quo—she'd help me with my reputation if I helped her win the election."

"What can you do? You can't even vote for her." Ruth squirted some purple styling goo on her hands and then ran them through my hair, twisting each curl around her finger until it formed a perfect ringlet.

The goo made my scalp tingle pleasantly, and I felt my shoulders start to relax. "I can spread what she told me about the Goodbodys, I guess. She can't tell people herself because it would look like a campaign smear. For all I know, it *is* a campaign smear."

"Why'd she trust *you* with the information, though?" Ruth squinted at me in the mirror and laughed at my offended expression. "Well, really. You avoid coming into town as much as possible. You hate talking to people."

"But she knows I'm friends with you—and with Eli, now that I think about it. She thinks he's *important*, and she's pretty certain he and I are a couple. She tried to sell us condoms," I said drily. I glanced over at the chair dryers to make sure the Raincoats, who were oiled and foiled and waiting for their highs to light, weren't listening.

Ruth followed my gaze in the mirror and grinned. "Don't worry, they can't hear anything. It's like a jet engine under one of those hoods. Anyway, aren't you and Eli a couple? Don't be offended just because Margie noticed."

"We're just friends," I said automatically. "And I'm not offended. Actually, I'm flattered she thinks I can still get pregnant."

Ruth giggled, then flicked on a blow dryer with a diffuser attachment and began gently drying my hair, taking care not to ruin the ringlets she'd formed. "So, are you going to?"

"What?" I said loudly over the whir of the dryer.

"Tell people."

I shook my head and she nudged me to hold still. I tried to hold my head steady as I answered. "I'm not sure it's true—she could be making it up just to put her opponent in a bad light. Why—do you think I should?"

"You should consider it."

I frowned. That wasn't the answer I was expecting. I was surprised Ruth had asked whether I would spread Margie's rumor at all—she was usually adamant that any gossip that passed through her chair was the truth, not conjecture. That

76

was part of why people were so eager to hear what she had to say. They knew it was information they could trust.

Ruth clicked off the dryer and spun my chair around to face her. "I'm just worried for you. Margie can hold a grudge. Her comment about your farm makes me think she'll have it out for you if you don't help her win. And you know how much weight she can throw around when she wants to. Remember Annaliese?"

I nodded. Annaliese was a chubby-cheeked girl with deep dimples who'd had the audacity to run against Margie for student council president back in high school. Margie managed to get her cut from the debate team by spreading a rumor that Annaliese stole M&Ms from the concessions stand, and then the whole school closed ranks against the poor girl. Maybe Annaliese had done it, maybe she hadn't, but all of the scrutiny led her to leave Honeytree High before the Homecoming dance. Margie got elected, and Annaliese homeschooled for the rest of her senior year. I was only a freshman at the time, but even I knew it wasn't right. And now Margie wasn't just an ambitious high school girl—she was the mayor and had connections all over the state. She could really do some damage...say, to a struggling small-business owner like myself.

Ruth finished drying my hair and turned me to face the mirror. She fixed a stray curl and surveyed her work with a satisfied nod, then applied a cloud of hairspray. "What do you think?"

"Shirley Temple ain't got nothing on me," I said. I hardly recognized my own reflection. My frizzy mane had been completely tamed—though probably not for long. At the moment, however, my curls looked smooth and shiny, like spun gold laced with silver. They'd be the envy of any princess,

Hollywood or otherwise. "This is red-carpet hair, Ruth. You could make a fortune in LA."

Ruth snorted. "And leave all this glamour behind?" She motioned around her little salon, at the strings of fairy lights and bohemian tapestries she had tacked to the walls and ceiling, the well-organized reception desk that doubled as a manicurist's station when Tambra wasn't taking time off for Spring Break, and the makeshift altar with candles and crystals and sage. "Never."

I stood and gave her an impulsive hug. "Thanks. For the hair, and for the advice. I think I know what I need to do now."

She nodded, her expression cautious and reserved. "I won't ask. But whatever you do, be careful."

Of course, she was right. And of course, I ignored her.

#

"Where is he?" I asked Preston. I scanned the comfortable interior of the church office, but there was no sign of Pastor Cal. Rows of leaflets with titles like "God In Your Marriage" lined one wall, and above them, a motivational poster reading "Keep Calm and Trust Jesus" hung next to a simple wooden cross. A cozy reading area with a bookshelf and easy chairs faced a large desk that held a name placard with Pastor Calvin's name on it. I noticed a few "Goodbody for Mayor" yard signs leaned up against the wall behind the desk, too.

Preston sighed and rubbed his red, puffy eyes. He looked like he'd been up all night. "I wish I knew. He's not answering his phone. I've had to cancel his whole afternoon. He was supposed to speak at the Friends of the Library meeting about the new literacy program he wants to spearhead as mayor. You don't happen to be a member, do you?" I shook my head, and he sighed again. "I was hoping you might be able to do some damage control."

"Sorry. I'm here to do some damage control myself."

Preston raised an eyebrow. "What kind of damage?"

I bit my lip as I tried to formulate my approach. Though he was Cal's campaign manager and spent a lot of time with the couple, I had no idea how much Preston might know about the Goodbodys' personal life. "Let's put it this way. I heard a rumor that I'm not sure is true. If it isn't, I'd like to know that."

"A rumor about Cal?"

I nodded. "I think it could affect the election if it starts to circulate. That's why I need to know if it's true."

Preston groaned and sank into one of the overstuffed green armchairs in front of the bookcase, resting his head in his hands. "I knew this was going to come up. I knew it. What have you heard?"

I shifted uncomfortably. "If you don't mind, I'd rather talk to Cal about it. I don't want to repeat a rumor if it isn't true."

"If it is what I think it is, it's true. Is it about their marriage?" Preston raised his head and looked at me. I nodded and he groaned. "I told him that Amelia was going to be trouble, but he swore he could manage her. He said they had an agreement—they were going to stay together until he got elected and held office for a year. Then they'd have an amicable divorce. I guess it doesn't matter now, though." He paused. "Who told you they were separated?"

"I was told in confidence, so I'd rather not say."

"It was Margie, wasn't it?"

Oops. Apparently, my line of questioning wasn't as discreet as I thought.

Preston shook his head disbelievingly. "I don't know why she bears such a grudge against Cal. He might be her political

79

rival, but she takes the rivalry way too far. Did you know she reported their dog to Animal Control for peeing on the tree by her house? It's not even in her yard, it's a city tree by the street."

"I don't want anyone to get in trouble. I just thought Cal should know the rumor circulating out there, so he could decide how he wants to handle it."

Preston snorted. "I'm pretty sure the only way to handle Margie Morrow is to beat her at the ballot box. Of course, that will be difficult without your discretion." Preston stood and adjusted his lapels, flashing a smile at me. His teeth were extremely white. He gestured to the stack of campaign signs behind the desk. "Would you like one? It'd be great to have a sign out in the Flats since so many people drive through there every day."

I ignored the offer—there was a reason no campaign signs peppered the stretch of highway between Honeytree and Duma. That's because the folks who lived in the Flats minded their own business and stayed out of small-town politics. I was surprised Preston was so blithe about the potential rumors, though. "You're not worried about what people will think when they hear about Cal and Amelia's problems?"

"Nope. I think Honeytree is rallying behind Cal," he said staunchly. "You saw the turnout yesterday. They love him. He's a good guy and he just lost the love of his life—sure, he and Amelia had their issues, but who doesn't? It makes him relatable, right?"

I shrugged. "Marriage trouble might. But lying about it and covering it up doesn't. Maybe you could get away with it in the anonymity of a big city, but in small towns, people don't appreciate being tricked. Especially not by their pastor."

A fleeting expression crossed Preston's face at my words. Anger? Shock? But it quickly settled into an ingratiating smile. He reached out to shake my hand. "Well, I'm glad *you're* a supporter. He'll need every bit of it in the coming months as he's learning the ropes in City Hall. I'll let him know you stopped by."

Before I knew it, I was back out on the sidewalk in front of the church. I had the answer I'd been looking for and more. Preston had all but admitted that Cal and Amelia were secretly split up at the time of the Easter Scramble. And how did he put it? He knew that Amelia would be trouble for Cal's campaign.

Except now, she wasn't.

Chapter 11

I walked back down the hill toward where my burgundy Suburban was parked in front of the sheriff's office, lost in thought. I wasn't sure how I'd clucked things up, but I had. Somehow, I had ruffled the feathers of both mayoral candidates in the space of an hour, when I'd only meant to smooth things over. Margie was sure to sabotage my business if I didn't spread the truth about Cal and Amelia. And Cal seemed likely to win the mayor's seat, so spreading rumors about him wouldn't win me any friends—or customers. Either way, Lucky Cluck Farm was in trouble.

Speaking of things that were clucked up...I winced as I saw Eli watching me from the sidewalk in front of his office.

"That was fast," he said when I crossed the street and reached for the driver's side door handle. I could only assume he'd been surveilling my little detour to the church and was irritated by my meddling. I braced myself for a scolding, but he just held out his hand.

I shook my head. "He wasn't there."

Eli withdrew his hand and frowned. "I thought you knew right where it was. It's got a thousand bucks in it—you can't just leave it laying around."

Oh, he meant the golden egg. I knew where *that* was...sort

of. "Not the egg. I couldn't find *him*. Pastor Cal. I haven't gone home for the egg yet." Truth be told, I'd forgotten all about it since Margie dropped the broken-marriage bomb.

Eli raised an eyebrow. "What do you want with Cal?"

I shoved my hands in my pockets sheepishly. "It's probably nothing."

"Liar." He barked a laugh. "There's no way Leona Landers—"

"Davis," I interrupted. As much as I wanted to shuck my ex-husband's last name, I hadn't been a Landers for more than thirty years. Plus, I didn't like Eli's assumptions that he knew what I would or wouldn't do. I'd changed a lot since I was his date to the Sadie Hawkins dance.

"Davis," he corrected, rolling his eyes. "There's no way *you* walked into a church looking for a pastor unless you had a good reason. You're not letting this Amelia thing go. Why not? You must know something." He eyed me appraisingly, his eyes lingering on my golden princess hairdo and slowly making their way down my entire body. I felt my chest and face flush under his scrutiny.

Darn it, he was right.

I yanked open the door of my car and slid into the driver's seat to escape, but he was too quick for me. Before I could put the Suburban into gear, he was sitting in the passenger seat beside me. Curse this old car and its lack of automatic door locks, too!

"Spit it out, Leona. What do you want with Cal?"

I gnawed my thumbnail and peeked him in my peripheral vision. His dark eyes were still searching my face—what he could see of it—and his expression was equal parts hopeful and earnest. He wasn't just asking me so he could turn it around and berate me. He really wanted to know what I was thinking.

I turned toward him. "Something's not right about all this. The pieces don't fit together. Think about it: Amelia died by the creek with the golden egg still in her hand. Even if she managed to fall face-first on a newt without getting wet or muddy, she hadn't been there long enough to be poisoned. Doc Morrow said it'd take half an hour to develop symptoms. She was only there for a few minutes—if that."

"Hm." Eli frowned and worried his lower lip, doing his own mental calculations. "She must have ingested the toxin earlier. Maybe she came into contact with a newt before she hid the eggs. Maybe she had an accident earlier that morning."

"It had to be before breakfast," I said, my shoulders relaxing now that Eli seemed to believe me. "Tammy Jenson said that Amelia was acting weird at the Rx Café that morning, remember—she ran for the bathroom right after she ate her eggs. She already had the poison in her system."

Eli's eyes opened wide. "You don't think Sara…?"

I shook my head firmly. "No. No. Again, it would take longer than that for Amelia to start feeling ill. Thirty minutes to develop any symptoms. If she was already queasy at breakfast, she ingested the poison at least half an hour before that."

He nodded thoughtfully. "So what was Amelia Goodbody doing before breakfast on Saturday morning?"

"That's the question I hope Pastor Cal can answer," I said. "If she fell down or had some other possible contact with a newt before breakfast, then we have our answer. But if she didn't?"

"Then maybe I'll owe you an apology for the tongue-lashing at the pharmacy." Eli winked.

"I think you do anyway." I started up the Suburban and paused, waiting for him to open the door and exit the vehicle. He didn't, though, just sat there smirking at me. I shooed him with my right hand. "Go on, get out."

"Oh, no. We're sticking together. There's no way I'm letting you talk to a suspect without me."

My jaw dropped. "What do you mean? Cal's a suspect?"

Eli nodded, and his face turned serious. "When a woman is killed, it's almost always the husband."

I stared at him. "But you were so convinced it was an accident!"

"I just follow the evidence. I admit, I gave the medical examiner's opinion a little more weight than yours. But the more I think about it, the more it seems likely that you were right and Amelia didn't accidentally lick an amphibian." Eli gave a little shrug. "Let's go find Cal."

"I don't even know where to start looking," I said as I pulled the car out onto the street.

"Luckily, I do."

I turned onto the highway. "Where's that?"

"My office."

I hit the brakes and the Suburban skidded to a stop in the middle of the road. Luckily for me, there was no traffic—pedestrian or otherwise—to witness my subpar driving, and the only traffic patrol in town was sitting in the passenger seat.

I turned to glare at Eli. "Are you serious? Cal Goodbody is in your office right now? Why didn't you say so?!"

"You didn't ask." Eli blinked innocently, making me wonder why the universe unfairly doled out long, curly eyelashes to men who don't even appreciate them.

I gritted my teeth and cranked the wheel so I could U-turn. Illegal, but so what? Eli could write me the ticket, and I'd show up in traffic court to prove it was his motherclucking fault.

This time I parked on the other side of the street in front

of Ruth's salon, getting out and slamming my door without a backward glance at Eli. He jogged around the car to catch up with me.

"He came to see the ME's report," he explained as we reached the sidewalk. "Just like you did."

I stopped at the curb. "Why didn't he get it faxed or emailed to him? He's family. The only reason I came in is because the county wouldn't issue me a copy unless I was related to Amelia somehow."

Eli shrugged as he walked past me and held open the door to the sheriff's office. "Good question. You'll have to ask him."

Cal had his back to the door, but I could tell from the way his shoulders were shaking as he slumped forward over the blue binder that he was crying. Not crying—sobbing. He raised his head when he heard our footsteps behind him and hurriedly dried his eyes on his plaid shirtsleeve. He closed the binder and twisted toward us, his face registering brief surprise when he saw me beside Eli.

"Sorry," he mumbled. He stood up from his seat and rocked on his feet, shifting his weight from heel to toe and back as he twisted his hands in front of him and then, realizing what he was doing, shoved his hands into his pants pockets. "This weekend has been such a roller coaster, and now this. I just don't understand how it happened."

The look on his face was almost too much to bear. He looked, in a word, broken.

"I'm so sorry for your loss," I murmured. It was a stupid, empty thing to say, and I'd already said the same thing to him yesterday at church, but the flash of gratitude on his face was almost worse than the grief. My whole chest ached for him.

"What don't you understand?" Eli asked gently, putting

a hand on Cal's shoulder. "Sit down a minute and we'll go through the report."

Cal nodded and sank back into his chair, dropping his head into his hands. "It's just—she was poisoned? With"—he raised his head and flipped open the binder, running his finger along the pages of the report until he found what he was looking for—"tetrodotoxin? Am I pronouncing that right? What is that?"

Eli took his seat behind the desk and folded his hands. "It's a naturally occurring poison produced by some animals. Amelia must have come into contact with it."

"But how?" Cal asked, bewildered.

He turned to me as though I might have the answer, but I shrugged at him. "We were hoping you knew."

"Walk us through her actions on Saturday morning," Eli said. He leaned forward over the desk toward Cal. "Did anything unusual happen? Anything outside her usual routine?"

"Nothing was *usual* about Saturday." Cal swallowed, shaking his head. "But I don't remember any animals. We had a meeting about the Easter Scramble, then had breakfast at the Rx Café, then split up to hide the treasure eggs. I never saw her again."

"What about before that?" Eli pressed. "What about at home? Did she do any work in the garden? Did she take a walk? Did she trip and fall? Did she eat or drink anything before you left the house that morning?"

Cal shook his head. "Not that I recall."

Eli sat back in his seat, his face grave. "Then we have a problem. A real problem."

Cal barked a humorless laugh. "Is that what you call it when your wife is poisoned to death? A real problem?"

"I'm sorry," Eli said automatically. "Forgive my phrasing. I only meant that if what you say is true, then Amelia's death may not have been accidental. And that's not something I take lightly."

"Unfortunately, we have another problem," I said, meeting eyes with Eli.

He frowned at me. "What's that?"

I drew up a chair next to Cal and directed my words to him. "You're lying."

Chapter 12

Cal stood up abruptly and backed away from me. Eli rose, glancing back and forth between me and Cal, his hand unconsciously going to his utility belt as though he might have to use something on it—to what? Defend me? Subdue me? A giggle rose in my throat at the thought of being handcuffed by Eli, but I pushed it down.

"What is she talking about, Cal?" Eli asked, his voice calm and level even as Cal's apparent agitation grew.

Cal ran his hands through his carefully coiffed hair, rumpling its smooth, even comb-marks. Then he rubbed his hand over his mouth and jaw and paced back and forth across the small office. "I don't know. I don't know."

"He doesn't really know what Amelia did on Saturday morning," I explained, keeping a close eye on him in case he cracked and decided to lash out at me. "He and Amelia weren't living together. The whole perfect couple thing was a farce. You didn't see her until the Scramble meeting, did you?"

He stopped in his tracks and stared at me, seemingly at a loss for words.

"I talked to Preston this morning," I added. "He told me you and Amelia had an arrangement. A year, right? A year after the election, and then you'd discreetly divorce."

At my words, Cal's whole body crumpled, and he collapsed into his chair again, groaning. "We *had* an arrangement. Past tense. But we made up on Friday night at the Chamber of Commerce cocktail party. We spent the night together for the first time in weeks."

Eli sat down carefully, a wary eye still on both of us. "I'm feeling a little out of the loop," he said, shooting a dark look in my direction. Whoops. "Do either of you care to fill me in?"

"He and Amelia were Splitsville," I said. "They were hiding it from everyone."

"We were back together." Cal jutted out his jaw and crossed his arms defiantly.

I rolled my eyes. "No, you weren't. You left the party separately."

"How do you—oh, never mind," Cal said. "We left separately, but it was just for show."

"That makes *zero* sense." Eli threw up his hands. "You both are making *zero* sense. Leona says your relationship was just for show and you say your separation was just for show. Which is it?"

I shook my head and shrugged. I was just as confused as he was. "Don't ask me."

"It makes perfect sense if you know Margie Morrow." Cal's tone was bitter. "She threatened to expose us—to tell everyone our marriage was a sham—if I didn't drop out of the mayoral race. She made the threat weeks ago, but at the party on Friday, she gave me an ultimatum: announce I was withdrawing my candidacy at the Easter Scramble, or she would tell everyone what we'd been hiding."

"You'd lose a lot of the town's goodwill if it came out," Eli observed. I rolled my eyes. Thanks, Captain Obvious.

Cal nodded. "If Margie spread her rumor—"

"You mean the truth," I broke in. "If she spread the truth."

"Whatever you want to call it. If it came out, I'd lose my wife, the election, *and* my pastorship. Everything," Cal finished sadly. "So I went to Amelia. I said, 'If I drop out of the race, will you take me back?' She never wanted to be in the public eye, anyway. That's why we split up."

Eli arched a skeptical eyebrow. "So she agreed?"

Cal nodded. "*We* agreed. I'd drop out of the race at the Easter Scramble, and she'd move back in with me. In that instant, I went from losing three out of three things I cared about most to winning two out of three. We spent Friday night together. Heck, I would have cooked her breakfast in bed on Saturday morning if we didn't have all the Scramble nonsense already planned. I wish I had just canceled everything and stayed home with her. Then she might have…"

"I don't buy it," I said.

"Be nice," Eli said reprovingly. "The man just lost his wife." Apparently, he'd bought Cal's story, hook, line, and sinker. Lucky for him, I wasn't so susceptible to Cal's brand of bait.

I ignored Eli's reprimand and focused on Cal. "If you were caving to Margie's demands, why pretend you were still separated when you left the party? Why keep up appearances when you'd been trying to hide your separation from everyone up until that point?"

"Oh. That." Cal glanced nervously at Eli as he stalled. "Well… the thing is…"

"The thing is, he didn't keep it hidden from everyone," Eli said sharply, as though he'd just realized it himself. "At least two people knew you and Amelia were split up: Margie and Preston. I suspect Doc Morrow probably knew, too. I can't imagine Margie would keep that a secret from him. So you were putting on a show for one of them."

"I didn't want Preston to know I planned to drop out, OK?" Cal snapped. "I knew he'd try and talk me out of it, so I made my little deal with Margie and then left the party as fast as I could. Amelia did the same. We met up later at home. And everything was perfect until—until she didn't show up at City Hall." Cal's cleft chin wobbled momentarily as he struggled to rein in his emotions.

My heart squeezed for him. I almost bought it.

Almost.

"So why didn't you withdraw your candidacy at the Scramble?" I asked bluntly. "You didn't need her to make the announcement. I was there—you didn't even try. And you didn't seem worried that Margie might spill the beans about your separation. It's almost like you knew Amelia was already dead and the rumor didn't matter anymore."

"Excellent question." Eli stilled as he waited for Cal to respond.

Cal's eyes went wide like a deer in headlights and he swallowed hard before answering. "Amelia and I decided to announce it at church on Easter Sunday instead. News media were covering the egg hunt, and I didn't want to detract from the good press by talking about the election on camera. The Scramble isn't about me, it's about the Honeytree community. I brought it up to Margie at the Scramble meeting that morning and luckily she agreed to give us another twenty-four hours to withdraw."

I squinted at him, trying to decide whether he was telling the truth or not. Pink spots burned high on his cheeks, but it was hard to tell if they were due to the heat of being a liar-liar-pants-on-fire, or due to the burn of my accusation. "Luckily for you, you mean. Now you still have a shot at winning the election. You still have two out of three things you want most, right? Your church and the mayor's seat."

"No," Cal said flatly. "Nothing compares to Amelia, and I resent your implication that I'd ever willingly give her up."

Eli shot me a look and motioned with his hand for me to settle down. That really ruffled my feathers, and I scooted my chair back and stood up. "I will not!"

"You will, or you'll have to step outside and cool off," Eli said, his attention still mostly on Cal. He slid a yellow legal pad toward himself and clicked his pen. "OK. Now that I have some sense of the events on Saturday, let's run through everything that you can remember Amelia touching on Saturday morning. I'm talking toothpaste, mouthwash, food, drink—everything."

I stood there a minute, watching and listening as Cal began rattling off a long list of products that Amelia applied to her face. Half of them sounded worse than tetrodotoxin.

"What's hyaluronic acid, anyway?" I asked.

Eli shushed me and motioned for Cal to continue. I felt the blood rush to my head. He was shushing me now that he was getting what he wanted from Cal, but if I hadn't been here with my nosy questions, he'd have nothing. He wouldn't have asked Cal anything at all, just sent him on his merry way after he viewed the ME's report.

That reminded me of my earlier question—why *did* Cal come into the sheriff's office to view the report at all, when he could have had a copy sent to him? I opened my mouth to ask, but Eli sensed my question coming and held up a finger to silence me.

A finger!

I held up a finger of my own. I'll let you guess which one.

Eli continued to ignore me, so I left, taking my question with me. Let's see if he got anywhere without my help.

Chapter 13

The flock was excited to see me when I got home, especially Boots, who'd been happily chilling in the bathroom sink. After I let her out and collected and sorted the afternoon eggs—my kitchen fridge was filling up fast—I let the rest of the flock out to forage in the yard while I sat on the porch, drank a cup of decaf, and watched them so they didn't wander too far or get swooped up by the red-tailed hawk that sometimes patrolled the Flats for roadkill.

Boots nabbed a few bugs in the yard before returning to hop in my lap and peck hopefully at the button on my jeans. Alarm Clock, my gorgeous Welsummer rooster that looked like he jumped straight off a box of Corn Flakes, flew up to roost on a fence post so he could keep a careful eye on his girls, too.

I had a handful of cockerels, too, the counterparts to the barnyard-mix and packing-peanut pullets. A small club of them acted as Alarm Clock's deputies, deferring to his leadership and keeping the pullets busy with their clumsy, teenage attempts at mating. I'd only kept the nice boys and sent the scrappy ones to live in Ruth's freezer, so everybody got along for the most part.

The flock fanned out under the apple trees, nipping off the sweet tips of grass blades and scratching at the roots to rustle up insects and worms. I hoped the greens and bugs would make their yolks even richer and more flavorful than they already were. In a few weeks, they'd be breakfast for everyone in town—just as soon as they forgot about what Amelia had for breakfast on Saturday.

Of course, nobody was likely to forget once they found out that she likely hadn't died by accident. I didn't have a chance to speak to Eli about it, but the more Cal talked, the more I'd begun to suspect him of slipping his wife some poison. Like Preston had put it, Amelia had been a real problem for Cal's campaign—and for his job as pastor, too, and his image as the golden boy of Honeytree.

Now that I thought about it, everything Cal did was underhanded—he'd pretended he and Amelia were together when they were separated, and then pretended they were separated when they were together. He'd promised his wife that he'd withdraw from the mayoral race and then pushed back the announcement—a little too conveniently to a date when she would be out of the picture. And for someone who'd supposedly been eager to end his candidacy, he'd stubbornly continued to campaign, even attending events the day after his wife died, when most people would have been seeking privacy to mourn.

I sipped my coffee as I pondered how to prove my suspicions. Maybe I could sneak into his house and find residue from whatever he'd used to poison Amelia. Where did they live? All I knew about their home life was that they had a dog—the one Margie had reported for peeing on her tree. That meant they probably had a fence, so I began mentally walking the streets in town, checking off those houses with unfenced yards and those whose occupants I already knew, trying to narrow down the possibilities.

There was a blue ranch by the high school that could be it—it was near enough to Margie's Seventies split-level that the Goodbodys might have walked their dog there. But it could also be the peach-and-brick number a few blocks in the opposite direction, near the road to the cemetery. Oh, who was I kidding? There were six or eight houses in between that fit the bill, too. Why waste time speculating on the address when I could just look it up in the phone book?

With a quick scan of the orchard to make sure my flock was sticking close to the house and not wandering near the road, I ducked inside to check the white pages. I found it under one corner of the armchair in the living room. I'd rescued the three-legged chair from a second-hand shop intending to replace all the legs but had never got around to it. I pulled out the phone book and wedged a dictionary under the leg instead.

I flipped through the whisper-thin pages until I got to the Gs. The Goodbodys weren't listed. Maybe they had an unlisted number, or maybe they were young enough that they didn't have a landline and only relied on their cell phones. It was shortsighted of them—the coverage in Honeytree was spotty at best. But if they were from a bigger city in Idaho, maybe Pocatello or Boise, they might be clinging to their urban ways.

Ruth would know their address. I pulled my phone out of my purse and was just about to text her to ask when my landline rang. I jumped about a foot in the air. I really, *really* hate being surprised. Flustered, I put down my cell and picked up the cordless phone, ready to tell off the telemarketer who'd so rudely interrupted.

"What do you want?"

"May I speak to Ms. Leona Davis, please?" The voice on

the end of the line was pleasantly neutral and clipped and surprisingly didn't sound like it originated in a foreign country.

"No, you may not. In fact, take me off whatever list you have my number on. I'm not interested."

"Oh, I think you are. I'm calling to inform you that your Oregon egg handler's license has been suspended pending investigation by the Oregon Department of Agriculture. All sales of eggs to retailers and eateries must cease, effective immediately, and cannot resume until you've undergone inspection. Your case number is eight-zero-one-zero. Please make note of it and use it for future communication with the department."

"Pardon?" I said scrambling for a pencil. "Can you repeat that?"

"The case number is eight-zero-one-zero. You'll receive a registered letter with your scheduled inspection appointment window."

I jotted "8101" in the margins of the phone book, my heart pounding in my chest. "How long will it take to get an appointment?"

"Law requires that your inspection occur within ten business days."

"Can you tell me why my license has been suspended?"

"Ma'am, the registered letter will include the original complaint." The voice on the phone sounded bored. "You can direct all further questions or requests to reschedule to the number at the bottom of the form. Thank you for your time."

Click. Dial tone.

I stood there a minute, stunned and staring at the droning receiver, until my head swam and I realized I was holding my breath. I let the air out in a rush and put the phone back in its base. Somehow, word had reached the state level that eggs from my farm had been involved in Amelia Goodbody's death. I shook my head wordlessly. This was getting out of control.

Outside, I heard Alarm Clock making a sharp series of warning cries—the sound he made when a hawk or owl swooped overhead, letting his ladies know to duck and cover. His warning was echoed by a chorus of other voices, his little army of cockerels passing the message throughout the orchard. I'd left them alone too long and a predator had targeted my flock.

I dashed for the door, dropping the phone book in my haste, and burst out onto the porch just in time to see my eighty-odd birds scattering in every direction as a frantic figure in a multicolored coat ran in circles in the orchard after them. What in the world...?

Then I saw Ruth's car in the driveway. Sure enough, another look at the person running around like a chicken with her head cut off confirmed that the long, rainbow patchwork coat belonged to Ruth, too. Her car coming down the driveway must have spooked the chickens, and now she was trying to round them up—but she was going about it the wrong way.

Instead of chasing after her in the orchard, I walked around her car to the barn, grabbed a bag of dried meal worms, and emerged. I shook the bag a couple of times by the chicken run and watched, bemused, as a horde of chicken heads swiveled to look at me simultaneously. Then a mad dash began, their little legs pinwheeling toward me as Ruth stood stunned under an apple tree, staring at me with her arms slack by her sides.

"How'd you do that?!" she hollered to me.

I flung a few handfuls of the crispy critters into the run and stepped back so the birds could charge inside. They poured chattering and flapping into the coop and jostled each other to get the best angle on the prize—except Boots, who I could tell apart from her sixty-nine identical sisters by the green zip tie around her right ankle and the fact that she stopped at my feet to peck up the few mealworms that I'd accidentally dropped rather than running to get the mother lode like the rest of the flock.

I nudged her with the toe of my shoe. "Go on—get inside."

Boots ruffled her feathers and dug her toenails into the dirt, refusing to budge, and clucked indignantly at me. I rolled my eyes and locked up the coop. "Oh, fine."

By then, Ruth had made it back to the house, and I joined her on the porch, Boots on my heels. Ruth swooped the hen up and tucked her under her arm, stroking Boots's head gently with her free hand.

"There you are, my little one. I was looking for you," she cooed. Then she looked up at me. "Sorry about that—I thought I could get them back toward the house but it was like trying to round up raindrops. How'd you train them to come back to the coop?"

"Doesn't take much to get those birdbrains in the palm of your hand—you just need the right bait." I held up the nearly empty bag of chicken treats and Boots successfully struggled hard enough toward it that Ruth set her down on the porch. I shook the last few mealworms out of the bag, along with a puff of bug-dust, for her to gobble up. We both watched the little hen chirp delightedly in between snapping up her newfound treasure.

"Your hair still looks good," Ruth observed, tucking a strand back into place. "I figured it'd be a mess by now."

"You were generous with the hair spray. Plus, I got stuck in town talking to Eli, so I haven't gotten much work done this afternoon."

"Stuck with *Eli*, huh? That must have been horrible." She wrinkled her nose mischievously.

"Oh, shut up and come inside. You want some tea? I'd offer you coffee, but I just finished off the pot."

"I can't stay. I just stopped by for a minute because I have an appointment to show the Sutherland place to some potential buyers!"

My eyebrows shot up. The blueberry farm next door had been sitting empty for months. Ruth was the listing agent, but there hadn't been much interest. That was the way with rural properties, especially ones as large and complex as that one, with acres of berry bushes, several outbuildings, and a hundred-year-old farmhouse. I knew from my own experience how much maintenance a farm like that required. People didn't usually want to take all that on when they were looking for a new home. It took a special buyer.

"They're from California," Ruth added. "Drove up here from the Bay Area to have a look at it. They want to pull out all the blueberries and plant grapes."

"Pinot fever," I said wryly. It seemed like everyone who moved here from our more affluent neighbor to the south had dreams of owning their own winery and replicating the success of famous Oregon vintners. They thought winemaking involved choosing pretty stemware and orchestrating pic-turesque views—they didn't realize all the drudgery that came with actual farming.

"Annnnnnd…" Ruth drew out the word hesitantly.

"And what?"

"They want to meet you. Is that okay?" She cringed,

anticipating my response. "They like to get a sense of the neighborhood synergy."

I laughed. "Neighborhood synergy? What does that even mean?"

"You know. The community."

"There is no community."

She rolled her eyes at me. "Of course there is."

"No, seriously. The main characteristic of the Flats *community* is that we all mind our own business. You know that. Good fences make good neighbors, don't turn around in my driveway, et cetera, et cetera." I didn't relish the idea of neighbors who wanted to collaborate. The whole point of moving up here was to be self-sufficient and avoid the scrutiny of judgy Californians, and now a couple of judgy Californians were going to move in next door.

Ruth pursed her lips. "Well, can you do me a favor and act friendly if I bring them over? Play up your little egg farm, your organic orchard, and so forth? They'll eat that up."

"I wish they would, literally," I muttered.

"What?"

"Eat my eggs. Nobody in town will, and now I've got the ODA breathing down my neck. Maybe I should sell to Californians who don't know any better."

"The ODA?!" Ruth checked the time on her phone. "Shoot. I want to ask what's going on, but it'll have to wait. I'll be back in an hour with my clients, OK? Promise me you'll be nice to them. I really need this sale. Things are tight for me right now."

Her anxious expression bored through any resistance I'd been developing to the idea. "Of course—anything for you."

Chapter 14

"We're picturing a retail store by the highway," the woman who Ruth had introduced as Kelly said, her hammered silver earrings glinting in her shiny auburn hair as she made an expansive gesture to the frontage of my property.

"Uh-huh," I said politely, not really listening to what she said.

"Wine tastings daily. Maybe a little vegan café with wine pairings," she said. Her husband, Sam, a tall man with the kind of carefully cultivated five o'clock shadow that was too perfect to be real, nodded beside her. Together, they looked like a magazine advertisement for an antidepressant: irritatingly natural, wholesome, and wealthy.

"We'd have an area inside for local farmers to rent shelf space. Sort of a mini French-style market, if you will," he explained.

I nodded. "I sell eggs."

The couple glanced at each other for a long moment. The woman finally replied. "We'd prefer not to stock animal products," she said gently. "But you could sell jams and jellies, things like that."

"Egg jam?" I looked at her, bewildered. "Egg jelly?"

The man laughed broadly like I'd told a good joke. "Well, I was thinking apple. Or you might discover raspberry or strawberry is more profitable. I'm sure you'll find your niche."

"I already have a niche—it's eggs." From behind them, Ruth shot me an apologetic look. I guess my face gave away my distaste for Sam's brand of condescension.

He nodded, looking up the driveway at my coop and the bobbing heads of the chickens inside. "About that…"

A long pause.

Kelly interrupted the silence. "What he means is that we're hoping to persuade you to change your focus. Why *chickens*"—she said it the way someone might say *maggots*—"when you have these beautiful trees?" She reached up her hand and brushed a row of apple blossoms, sending a cascade of pink petals fluttering to the ground.

Don't hit her. Don't hit her, for Ruth. I slid my clenched fist into the pocket of my jeans and pasted on a fake smile. "Um… because I want them? And I already have a productive flock and a brand-new coop. What's your problem with chickens, anyway?"

They exchanged another glance.

"Well…" Sam squinted into the distance, as though he were trying to find just the right words.

Once again, Kelly filled the empty space. "The fact is, we're concerned about the smell."

"And the view," Sam added. "We'd prefer an unobstructed view of the vineyard from the farmhouse, and right now your chicken enclosure is a bit of an eyesore."

Ruth's eyes went so wide I could see the whites all around her pupils as she pantomimed frantically for me to zip my lips. Unfortunately, I was all out of zips.

"Let me get this straight. You want to build a store that's half on my property?" Kelly nodded eagerly, her expression bright, so I continued. "And you want to rent space in the store—the store on my property—back to me, so I can sell jam that I don't make instead of eggs that I do make?"

"Mhm, that would be ideal."

"And you want me to knock down my brand-new chicken coop and—what? Cull the chickens who live in it? Chop, chop?" I made a slicing motion across my neck.

Sam frowned. "We didn't say anything about killing animals. You could *rehome* them."

"All so you can see your imaginary vineyard." My voice gained a dangerous edge. "And what do I get out of all this? The privilege of being your neighbor?"

Kelly tittered, as though I'd made a joke instead of asking a critical question. Then, as she saw the grim set of my jaw and realized I was serious, she began blinking rapidly. "Well, you'd be part of a new, dynamic cohort of next-generation producers. You'll be able to rub shoulders with agritourists and wine aficionados from all over the globe."

"Right. I'm sure the caliber of my social media followers would increase," I said sarcastically.

"Exactly! Wonderful! I'm so glad you understand!" She clasped her hands, her expression relieved, and turned to Ruth. "I think this is going to work out great. Let's go back to your office and draw up the paperwork. Don't you think it's perfect, honey?"

Ruth, who should have been over the moon about an eager buyer, chewed the inside of her cheek as she stared at me, searching my face for answers. I had a few answers I could give. For example, I'd rather move back to snobby Beverly Hills than live next to Jam and Jelly, here.

But I knew Ruth really needed the sale, too. Honeytree was

small, and properties didn't come up for sale very often. She relied on both her businesses to pay the bills. I couldn't deny her a commission that might be half her income for the year just because my new neighbors might be irritating. I could endure twenty or thirty years of bad neighbors for Ruth. I wouldn't do it for anyone else.

I gave a quick nod. "Good luck," I said to the couple. "Make sure you stop by for some coffee after you move in."

The woman flashed a smile at me as she clutched her husband's arm, and he beamed down at her. "You're finally going to have your Tuscan hideaway, honey," he said. "Bonus, we don't even have to learn Italian. That's the only reason we didn't move straight to Italy," he added to Ruth.

Ruth smiled politely. "You might want to learn French to source your vines."

The woman waved her hand. "We'll hire someone for that."

"Spanish could be helpful for hiring seasonal vineyard labor, as well." Ruth gave me a sly look out of the corner of her eye. What was she doing? If I didn't know better, she was trying to sabotage her own sale.

Jam and Jelly weren't derailed. "We'll only hire locals," the woman declared. "It'll be good for our brand, anyway."

"Wonderful," Ruth said, in a tone that belied her words. "Now let's go over some details. Soil testing will run in the thousands—would you like to get that started?"

"Yes, right away," Jam said, nodding.

"OK. And you'll want to know about the water rights—this property doesn't have any irrigation rights to the creek, and the state of Oregon prohibits rainwater collection. You'll likely have to drill a new well to support a vineyard."

"Fine," Jelly chirped. "Where do we sign? I want to be

drinking a glass of my own wine come next fall."

Ruth bit her lip. "That's not going to happen. I'm no vintner, but I know it takes at least three years for pinot grapes to mature. And the yields will be low for the first few years. You'll want to have a plan for the carrying costs, plus the initial investment in site prep and vines, building your retail space… *if* your permit is approved. There are a lot of unknowns here."

Jelly blinked, her giddy expression fading. She glanced to her husband. "Honey? Is that true?"

He shifted uncomfortably, looking back and forth between his wife and Ruth. "Of course. I knew that. I've done my research." Judging by his uncertain tone, he definitely did not know that and had definitely not done his research.

Jelly frowned. She must have sensed his lack of confidence, too. "Maybe we should keep looking for a vineyard that already has grapes planted," she said doubtfully.

Ruth nodded. "Maybe you should."

I couldn't believe she was letting this deal slip through her fingers. She had no fiduciary responsibility to these people—she was the listing agent, not their buyer's agent! While I'd rather Jam and Jelly got on a plane to Europe instead of moving to the Flats, I really wanted Ruth to make the sale.

"You could purchase pinot grapes from someone else for the first few years," I offered. "A lot of people grow them who don't have winemaking facilities. You could focus your efforts on the wine side while you wait for your own grapevines to mature."

The sparkle came back into Jelly's eyes, and Jam looked at me gratefully. "That's exactly what I had in mind," he said. "I'm glad you picked up on that."

I suppressed an eyeroll. How like a man to take credit for

my idea. "Great plan," I said sweetly.

Ruth sidled closer to me so she could poke me in the ribs without them noticing. "Stop," she murmured. "I'm trying to help you here."

"Same," I said through my fake-smiling teeth.

Jelly stood on tiptoe to plant a kiss on Jam's movie-star stubble. Then she turned to us. "We want to get an offer in as soon as possible," she said. "Can we sign the papers here?"

"Let's sign over dinner," Ruth said. "Why don't I meet you at Hopdale Brewery in Duma in about an hour? That'll give me a chance to get everything drawn up for you."

"Perfect!" Jelly trilled. "Isn't it perfect, honey?"

"Perfect," he echoed.

#

The minute they left, Ruth and I were at each other's throats.

"Why'd you throw them a life preserver with that whole 'buy your grapes' thing?!" Ruth demanded.

I sucked in my cheeks. "Why'd you suddenly throw up all those barriers to sale once you had them on the hook? It's almost like you don't *want* to pay your mortgages."

She crossed her arms and gave me a sulky look. "I could say that same of you. You seem pretty determined to put your egg farm out of business."

At the mention of my eggs, my shoulders sagged. "I'm probably going out of business, anyway. The state suspended my egg handler's license. Jam and Jelly might be doing me a favor by asking me to shut down my chicken operation."

"Jam and Jelly." Ruth giggled at my nicknames for the couple. Then she blinked. "Wait, what? Why was your license suspended?"

"I'll know more when I get the official paperwork, but I'm

guessing it was due to Amelia's death. It's going to be tough to shake that association, whether I get my license back or not. And in the meantime? I have two fridges full of eggs that nobody wants to eat. At least if I made jams and jellies, they'd last a little longer on the shelf."

Ruth put her arm around me, and I slumped against her a little. She chuckled and propped me back up. "You can't give up so easily. Chickens are your dream."

"Maybe a dream that I can't make a reality, though," I said glumly.

She squeezed my shoulder as we walked back through the orchard to the house. "Don't worry, at dinner I'll make sure those two bail on building their Tuscan retreat in the Flats."

I whirled on her. "Don't you dare! I promised my best friend I wouldn't let anything come between her and this deal, and I intend to keep that promise. Her business needs to succeed as much as mine does, and I swear, if you cluck this up for her, I am never speaking to you again!"

Ruth stopped suddenly at the foot of the porch steps, her forehead creased and her eyebrows drawing together. "You mean it? You really want me to let them to put in an offer?"

I looped my arm around her and offered a squeeze of my own. "I do. If you let this fall through, we might both be out of business, and one of us has to pay our mortgage in case the other one needs to move in."

She laughed, stopped and looked at me, then laughed again. "You know what? Suddenly going broke doesn't sound so bad. But only if you're sure you don't mind living next to these people for the rest of your life."

I snorted. "You know as well as I do that they're not going to last that long in the wine business. They just want to tell people they run a winery, not do the actual work."

"They might steamroll you," she said worriedly. "They have strong personalities."

"Steamroll *me*?! Don't worry, I can take care of Jam and Jelly. You just make sure that farm gets sold and the commission check has your name on it."

Ruth grinned at my nickname for the couple. "Let's make a bargain. I'll sell them the blueberry farm, and you make sure that by the time they move in, your egg business is booming so big that the *community dynamic* requires you to keep your birds."

I nodded. "You got yourself a deal. And a dozen eggs. Let me go get you a carton." I took the stairs two at a time and swiftly returned with a carton of eggs from the porch fridge. I handed them to Ruth, and she took them with a thoughtful expression on her face.

"You know," she said, reflexively opening the carton to check the eggs for cracks and then closing it again, "I'm pretty sure you don't need an egg handler's permit to sell directly to individuals, so any cease-sales order from the ODA only puts the kibosh on wholesale orders. And you're not making those sales anyway right now. What if you just sell them one carton at a time?"

Hope sprouted in my chest. I hadn't really thought about selling to individuals. It had seemed more lucrative to sell all my eggs in one or two large wholesale orders, but at this point, I'd take every five bucks I could get to put toward chicken feed. "That's not a terrible business plan. It'd at least hold me over until the Rx resumes their regular order."

Ruth poked me in the ribs again. "Of course it's not a terrible plan—I'm a successful entrepreneur, remember? I'm a member

110

of the motherclucking Chamber of Commerce."

My mind was already whirring so loudly, making a mental list of people I knew who'd buy from me, that I hardly heard her retort. "Now I just need to find enough people willing to take a chance on my eggs."

Ruth snapped her fingers. "Farmers market. This week is the first one of the season. Get a booth! That's my last piece of free advice. Any more and I'll have to charge you a consulting fee." She winked at me.

"Then I'm charging you for these!" I snatched the carton of eggs back from her and her mouth dropped open. I giggled at her expression and held them back out to her. "Just kidding. I think Boots would move out if I charged you for eggs. And at this point, I'd pay *you* to take these off my hands."

Chapter 15

Tuesday, Day 4

The next morning, I was waiting on the sidewalk when a freshly curled and pressed Margie Morrow unlocked the door to City Hall. She wore a royal purple skirt-suit with a huge silk peony quivering on her left lapel. "Mayor of Honeytree, OR" was embroidered in gold on the jacket's breast pocket. Now that was confidence. She obviously wasn't worried about needing a new wardrobe after next month's election.

I tried to enter the building, but Margie moved to block the doorway, raising a drawn-on eyebrow at me. "I'm surprised to see you here, Leona."

"Why's that?" I raised my eyebrows right back. "Isn't this the place to register for a table at the farmers market?"

She smiled, her fuchsia lipstick cracking at the edges, but the smile didn't reach her eyes. "I'm disappointed in you. I really am."

I snorted and squeezed past her into the small lobby. Honeytree had apparently bought grim gray office furniture in bulk—the décor in here was the same as in Eli's office. The only difference was the "Life is Sweet in Honeytree" banner that hung above the reception desk. I spun the circular rack of forms, scanning it for the farmers market application. "Sorry you feel that way."

"I expected to hear more around town about Pastor Cal's... situation," she said behind me, with all the tact of a pig at a trough.

I spotted the form I was looking for and plucked it out of the rack before turning to face her. "I did a little investigation after we talked. Turns out, the situation wasn't as simple as you made it out to be, *Marge*."

She made a face at the nickname. "I haven't the foggiest idea what you're talking about."

"You kind of left out the part where you were attempting to blackmail Cal to drop out of the race." I grabbed a pen off the desk and sat down to fill out the form.

"I never did any such thing." Margie sniffed. "I only suggested *politely* that he might want to avoid the scandal when the details of their marital situation came out. If my years in politics have taught me anything, it's that things always come out eventually."

"They do if you plan to announce them at the Easter Scramble." I filled in the blanks for name and address on the farmers market form, then checked the box next to "small local farm" with a flourish. "I think you moved from 'polite suggestion' to 'blackmail' when you put a deadline on his decision."

"People deserve to know," she said indignantly. "You can't have informed voters without information, right? And Cal came around to that opinion, too. He agreed to withdraw rather than tell people the truth."

I signed the bottom of the form and handed it to her. "Is it still fifteen bucks?"

She put on a pair of purple reading glasses from the desk and scanned the paper. Then she gave it back to me. "You forgot to write down your egg handler's license number."

I flushed. "It's not required."

"It certainly is!"

"Check the code, Margie. I don't need it to sell to consumers, only to restaurants. I'll wait while you go look it up." I crossed my arms and sat back in the uncomfortable chair.

She pursed her lips and snatched the paper out of my hands. "Fine. I'll check it later. But if your application is declined, the fifteen-dollar fee is nonrefundable."

"Fine," I echoed. I plucked a wrinkled ten and five out of my wallet and smoothed them a little before handing them to her. "Will I be able to sell on Thursday?"

A small smile quirked the corner of her mouth. "You seem very confident that you'll be approved."

"I know the law," I said, rising to my feet.

"This week, I may decide to limit the number of sellers." That annoying eyebrow arched again. This woman was put on earth to test me. "I can do that, you know. Unless…"

I sighed. "Unless what?"

"Unless Pastor Cal makes good on his word to withdraw from the race. It concerns me that he didn't follow through on our agreement—much as it concerns me that you didn't." Her voice was all sugar. So this was how Margie Morrow got things done. "Maybe we can solve both problems if I give you a little ammunition."

I blinked. "What're you talking about?"

She sat down in the chair next to me. "Don't you think it's

114

a little convenient that the second Cal's secret was going to be exposed, Amelia dropped dead? Sort of solved that little problem for him, didn't it? Now he's the grieving widower instead of a liar and a fraud."

I'd had the same suspicion myself, but I wasn't going to give Margie the satisfaction of knowing that. "Here's the funny thing. Your little attempt to expose their broken marriage actually drove them back together. They reconciled that night at the cocktail party. They spent Friday night together. So there's nothing to tell, Margie. He's not a liar. He was happily married—at least for Amelia's few final hours. I won't spread your poison any further than this waiting room."

I rose to leave, but Margie nabbed my sleeve and pulled me roughly back down into my seat. She leaned toward me so close I could see her powdery pores. "He *is* a liar," she hissed, her hot breath hitting me like a hurricane. You know, the kind of hurricanes that come in big cups with straws? "You don't know the whole story, but you have to trust me. The town needs to know the truth about him."

I barked a laugh and yanked my arm away so she lost her grip on my shirt. "Why in the world would I trust *you*? I have no reason to. You're a blackmailer who's trying to pressure me into sabotaging an election that you're probably going to lose otherwise. That's cheating, Margie. Don't you think Honeytree should know *that*, too?"

Margie's mouth dropped open and she blinked rapidly. "You have it all backwards!" she stuttered. "Cal threatened to blackmail *me*, not the other way around!"

"Right." I stood again and this time she didn't pull me back down. "Now I remember. Everyone is bad except you. My eggs are dangerous, Pastor Cal is a fraud and a blackmailer, and Annaliese stole candy from the concessions stand back in high school. Do I have that right?"

"She did," Margie said staunchly. "I saw her do it. We were working the concessions stand together. They found the evidence in her locker the next day!"

"Why didn't you stop her, then?"

Margie pressed her lips together and shook her head. "I don't remember why. I was probably scared I'd get in trouble, too."

"Oh gosh, what could your reasoning be?" I snapped my fingers. "Oh, I've got it—you knew it'd be more advantageous for your student council run if Annaliese was caught than if you stopped it from happening to begin with. And congrats, you were right. You ruined her life and you stole the election. And now you're trying to do the same thing again, and I'll be darned if I'm going to let you manipulate me into helping you."

Margie blinked rapidly. "Manipulate you?!"

"'You don't know the whole story. You have to trust me,'" I mimicked. "Right. You can't tell me the *real* reason, and why not? Because there is no reason except your naked ambition."

Margie tilted her head to the side, considering me—or maybe considering what to do with me. Then she held up my farmers market form and slowly tore it in half. She tossed the pieces in the wastebasket beside the desk and waved my fifteen bucks at me. "I'm sorry to say that your application has been declined, Leona. Better luck next time."

And then she turned her back on me.

The nerve!

I marched out the door, turned sharply right, and marched into the sheriff's office where Eli was on the phone with someone. I steamed quietly until he hung up.

"Couldn't go a day without me, huh?" He put his hands

behind his head and leaned back in his chair, giving me one of his patented George Clooney grins. Well, that strong jaw and good hair weren't enough to distract me.

"I want to report a crime."

He sat forward, looking surprised, and scrambled for his computer keyboard. "OK, I'm listening—what happened?"

"Margie Morrow just stole fifteen bucks from me!" I pointed to the west side of the room, in the direction of City Hall. I hoped my raised voice made it through the wall to Margie's ears.

Eli rolled his eyes. "Come on, now. You don't really want me to write that on a report, do you? I have a tough time believing Doc and Marge are that hard up that she'd fleece you for a few dollars."

"She took my money, knowing full well she wasn't going to approve my application. That's stealing," I said stubbornly.

Eli folded his hands like some kind of guru. "I sense some anger."

"You must be psychic." I rolled my eyes. "You better believe I'm angry. She only denied me a spot at the farmers market because I refused to do what she asked."

"Let me get this straight. You applied for the farmers market, which cost fifteen dollars? Then you didn't comply with Margie's terms, and she denied your application."

I nodded.

"Well, that sounds like she was exercising her discretion as mayor, not stealing."

"It's not like she was asking for something reasonable!" I said hotly. "Her terms involved lying!"

Eli frowned. "About what?"

"About Cal Goodbody, of course. She's upset that I didn't tell

117

everybody that he and Amelia were secretly split up. That's why she's holding my farmers market application hostage."

"Well, they were split up," Eli said, ever reasonable. "I understand that you might not want to spread it around town in the wake of the tragedy, but that's hardly a lie."

"It *is* a lie—according to Cal, they got back together before Amelia died, remember? But when I told Margie that, she kept pushing me, saying she knew other reasons that Cal was a liar and a fraud. And then she got really desperate and claimed that Cal was blackmailing *her* rather than the other way around. I think she's gone off the deep end." I shook my head. "She really will do anything to win this election."

Eli frowned. "That does sound serious. Maybe more serious than pocketing fifteen bucks."

"Easy for you to say. It's not your money," I grumbled.

He stood up and grabbed his uniform jacket from a hook behind the desk. "Walk over with me. Let's see how truthful Margie's accusations really are. Maybe she was just throwing her weight around in a moment of desperation, but maybe she was telling the truth—maybe there's more to Pastor Cal than meets the eye."

Chapter 16

I grudgingly followed Eli out the front door of the sheriff's office. I knew what would happen once we got inside City Hall. Marge-in-Charge would point to the fine print saying my application fee was nonrefundable. Eli would side with her, because his job is all about enforcing the fine print. Then she'd deny what she'd said about Cal blackmailing her, because who would admit to that? And Eli, already on her side, would believe her.

Eli held the door open and, dreading the sight of Margie's smug expression, I dragged my feet over the doorsill. I braced myself for some of her inane chit-chat, but instead I heard Eli draw in his breath sharply behind me. Then he jostled me aside as he made a dash for what I realized was a prone figure on the floor.

I froze at the sight. Margie was splayed out in front of the reception desk, two paper cups of coffee splashed across the floor in front of her, a half-eaten doughnut slowly soaking up the liquid. Eli skidded through the mess to kneel at Margie's side and check her pulse. He looked back over his shoulder at me as he began chest compressions.

"Go through the back"—he jerked his head toward the door behind the desk—"and tell Jasmine to bring her kit. Hurry!"

I shook myself and did as he asked. Jasmine—the paramedic who'd worked on Amelia when I found her—didn't ask questions, just grabbed a bag and followed me out of the fire station and back into City Hall. Her face registered shock when she saw Margie lying there.

"What happened!?"

"No pulse," Eli said tersely, punctuating his words with chest compressions. "Can you take over?"

She shook her head, slowly backing up as she held her kit in front of her like a protective shield. "Oh no…no way. Let me go get the bag."

Eli stopped what he was doing to stare at Jasmine, and I wanted to scream *Keep going! Don't stop!* "What do you mean, no way? You're obligated to help!"

Jasmine jutted out her chin, her cheeks flushing. "I'm not obligated if it puts me in mortal peril. Those are the rules of duty in the manual."

Eli threw up his hands. "There's no peril here, Jaz."

"Oh yeah? Tell that to Aaron. He's still in the hospital. I'm not putting my mouth on no poison after seeing him go through that, thank you very much."

"This isn't the same—she probably just had a heart attack," Eli said, resuming chest compressions that jolted Marge's whole body. I felt every one of them deep in my core.

Jasmine pointed to the soggy doughnut a few inches from Margie's right hand. It had a big bite out of it. "Last I heard, cream filling doesn't cause heart attacks. She must have eaten whatever Amelia did."

"I don't think the poison works that fast—" I began, but Eli cut me off.

"Come on—Marge needs you!" he snarled at Jasmine, but

she just shook her head even more firmly.

"Seems like you're doing fine. I'll get the van. I'll drive, you can bag her." She tossed the kit toward Eli and backed all the way to the door, fumbled the handle behind her, and left City Hall the way she came. Eli swore, took a deep breath, and began mouth-to-mouth.

Visions of Amelia's body rose in my mind, causing my stomach to roil. I couldn't watch this. Not again. I trained my eyes on the floor and edged carefully around Eli and Marge. Eli finished administering the breaths and rummaged through Jasmine's kit, looking for something. He paused to glance up at me. "It's OK if you need to wait outside. Really."

I couldn't get out of there fast enough. As I stumbled to the door and the sweet relief of the sidewalk, I tripped over one of the coffee cups on the way out. It rolled toward the door and I caught a glimpse of the logo printed on the side.

Rx Café — Good for what ails you.

Any other time, this wouldn't be notable. The Rx was the only place in town with takeout coffee, after all. But today—today it was notable. Because the Rx Café wasn't even open. That meant only one thing: Sara herself had brought the coffee to City Hall. And when Margie collapsed, Sara had run away.

I looked back, panicked, at Eli. He'd somehow managed to find a breathing bag and had affixed the mask to Margie's face. Even though I knew Margie couldn't have ingested the same poison as Amelia—she was fine when I was in City Hall only a few minutes earlier—I was relieved that Eli wasn't giving her mouth-to-mouth anymore. If Margie had been poisoned, and Eli had been exposed...

Well, I didn't even want to think about it.

121

I heard and then saw the ambulance pull up to the curb and Jasmine hopped out, her face tense and alert. "Clear the walkway, please," she said tersely as she passed me.

Her words jolted me into action. I had to find Sara. I jogged down the sidewalk toward the Rx. She had to be there—where else would she run? And if she wasn't at the café, I could ask Doc if he'd seen her...and tell him that his wife might be dead. Ugh.

I slumped against the café's doorframe, trying to catch my breath as I rapped on the door. A "CLOSED" sign hung in the window with a paper explanation taped above it: "Restaurant will re-open May 1. Sorry for the inconvenience."

I waited a few beats, and when Sara didn't come to the door, I cupped my hands to the glass to see inside the dim interior. There were no signs of life inside. Though the tables were set as though Sara expected a service, the kitchen lights were off. Only the red light on the coffee pot glowed ominously from behind the counter.

She *had* made coffee today. My heart hammered in my chest, and it wasn't from my jog down the sidewalk.

I strode briskly into the pharmacy and braced myself to deliver the news to Doc that Margie was dead—and possibly had been poisoned. A crash met my ears, and then Doc sprinted out of the pharmacy booth and past me with something in his hands. I wouldn't have believed that old Eeyore could move so fast if I hadn't seen it myself. I barely had time to say, "Margie..." as he flew past me. He held up whatever he had in his hands, as though I knew what that meant, and then ran down the street.

I stood there a minute, staring out the door and imagining the scene Doc was going to come upon when he pushed through the door to City Hall. But how did he know something was going on there, when Eli and I had only just found Margie's body? Someone must have told him. Jasmine? Or...

I turned back toward the pharmacist's booth and sure enough, there was Sara standing behind the counter, twisting her tattooed hands together. She winced when I caught sight of her, her eyebrows drawing together worriedly.

"I know what you're thinking," she said. "You're thinking it was my fault."

I gave a noncommittal shrug. "You have to admit, it doesn't look good. You bring Margie coffee, and then she immediately keels over."

Sara looked like she was going to burst into tears. "She didn't even drink the coffee! She had one bite of doughnut and—" She squeezed her eyes shut as a tear slipped down her cheek. "She choked out 'get Doc' and I so ran down here. I ran as fast as I could, I swear. When I told Doc what happened, he tore apart the place looking for her Epi-Pen. I only hope he got it to her in time. She's allergic to nuts," Sara added, motioning to the sign posted in the window, though it wasn't visible to us from the inside. I remembered what it said, though.

No peanuts. No tree nuts. No wingnuts.

Now the sign made more sense. And now I understood what Doc had held up to show me: Margie's Epi-Pen. Margie must have recognized the signs of anaphylaxis before she passed out. Before her heart stopped. Even though I didn't know whether Margie would live or not, I felt a strange sense of relief knowing that she hadn't been poisoned. That meant Eli hadn't been exposed to a toxin like Aaron Alpin had been—and Eli wasn't allergic to nuts, as far as I knew.

"I have to throw the rest of these out," Sara declared. She

marched over to the little table near the sink and scooped up a pink box. "They shouldn't even be in here. I just assumed, because Doc had them in the shop, that they were safe!"

I realized she meant the doughnuts that must be inside the box. "Wait, *you* brought Margie the doughnut, too? Not just coffee?"

Sara nodded, her chin wobbling as she held the pink box. "I did. But it didn't have nuts! The whole box is Boston cream, look!" Sara flipped open the lid. It was full of rows of round, fluffy pastries with shiny chocolate glaze. No nuts in sight. "I brought Doc a coffee, and then he said I should bring some to Margie, too. To butter her biscuit, he said. He gave me the doughnut to take with me. I thought it would help...but it didn't, obviously. There's no way, now..." Her voice cracked and trailed off, and I couldn't help feeling a pang of sympathy. Sara was trying to be helpful, and instead ended up in the middle of another catastrophe, poor thing. As if she didn't have enough problems.

"No way, what?" I asked. "Why did Margie's biscuit need buttering?"

Sara ducked her head, her voice thick with emotion. "I can't make the rent this month because of everything with Amelia. I came to ask Doc for an extension, but he said he couldn't make the decision without Margie's approval. He said her word was final, so I went to City Hall. But I didn't have a chance to ask."

I frowned. "Closing for a few days is enough to bust your budget for the whole month?"

Sara nodded. "Things were tight already. Why do you think I've been taking on side gigs? No sane person gets up at four a.m. to run a breakfast service and then stays up until midnight to cater a cocktail party." She frowned at the doughnut box in her hands, flipped the lid closed, and headed for the connecting door between the pharmacy and the café.

I'd almost forgotten that Sara had been at the cocktail party when all the blackmail business with Amelia and Cal had been going down. Maybe she'd overheard some of the conversations that night and could sort out what had really happened, since I couldn't exactly ask Margie now.

I glanced out the door at the empty street, torn between minding the empty pharmacy until Doc returned or following Sara. I opted for the latter. I turned the deadbolt on the front door so no passersby could drop in and nab medications from the pharmacy shelves, flipped the sign to "closed," then traced Sara's footsteps to the Rx.

In the darkened restaurant, I heard the back door creak open, the crash of the dumpster lid outside, and then the door open and close again. Bye-bye, secret-peanut doughnuts. Sara returned and, seeming unsurprised to see me standing there like a burglar caught red-handed, scrubbed the dumpster grime off her hands at the sink.

"I guess I have to kiss the café goodbye," she said over her shoulder. "Amelia always said I should go somewhere with a better food scene, anyway. She said this town would never appreciate what I had to offer."

I swallowed hard. For some reason, her words stung me, like I was the one who would be kissing my dream goodbye. "Building a business is hard. You shouldn't give up, though." I said it as much for me as for her.

She turned to face me and leaned against the sink. "Do you think Amelia was right?"

I tilted my head, considering the idea. Sara's food was comfortable—recognizable, easy to pronounce and understand—but she took it to another level, using the freshest and most delicious local produce available. She made every element, even down to the white bread under her egg salad, the most delicious it could be. I couldn't speak for everyone, but I certainly appreciated what the Rx Café had to offer. "No, I don't. People in Honeytree have taste buds the same as the folks in Portland. We like good food, too."

"There are more people in Portland, though. More people means more customers, and more customers means more income."

"More people means more competition, too," I pointed out. "Here you only have the Greasy Spoon to worry about, and Ed has a whole different thing going on over there. Amelia isn't from around here, so she doesn't necessarily understand the *community dynamic*." I borrowed Jam and Jelly's phrase with no small measure of satisfaction.

"Didn't," Sara said, her eyes downcast.

"Pardon?"

"Amelia *didn't* understand. Past tense."

"Oh, right." I sighed. "I didn't know you two were friends. You seem so…different." I couldn't help glancing at Sara's tattoos and punky hairdo, so different than Amelia's starched and pressed pastor's-wife image.

"Well, we were," Sara said defensively, crossing her arms. "We got really close in the last few weeks, since…" She trailed off, then shook her head. "I'll miss her, that's all."

"Since she and Cal separated?" I guessed.

Her eyes widened. "You knew?"

"Margie told me."

Sara's eyes narrowed. "Of course she did," she spat. "If one good thing comes out of her death, it'll be that she can't spread her lies around town."

I hoped Sara was wrong. As much as I disliked Margie, I didn't think anything good would come of her death. Whatever sympathy I'd felt for Sara's predicament evaporated like steam off manure. "What was Margie lying about? It was true they were having problems, wasn't it?"

"Problems *she* created!" Sara blurted out, color rising in her cheeks. "She was blackmailing them—that's why they split up! Amelia swore me to secrecy, but now that she's gone, I guess I don't have to keep that promise."

I racked my brain, trying to put the timeline together. How could Margie have caused their breakup, if their breakup was what she was using to blackmail Cal into quitting his campaign? It didn't make sense. "She told me that they were blackmailing *her*."

"That's rich," Sara said bitterly. "They were fine until Margie stuck her nose in their business. They had nothing against her."

"Why didn't they just get divorced and be done with it?" I'd be the first one to say that divorce was no picnic, but it was certainly better than sticking it out in an unhappy marriage. Trust me, I'd tried both, and divorce was *so* much better.

Sara stared at me, her expression confused. "What did Margie tell you, exactly?"

"The truth. She said Cal and Amelia weren't happily married. That they were living separately, not as man and wife, and were hiding it from everyone. Honestly, it seems like no big deal to me, but I guess for a pastor who's running for mayor, it's not a great image." I shrugged.

Sara shook her head disbelievingly. "She's more of a snake than I thought. I should have slipped peanuts into her pastries months ago."

My heart leaped and I took a step backward. Had Sara just admitted to poisoning Margie on purpose? As if to underline my fears, the ambulance siren began to wail down the street, the sound fading as it headed down the highway toward Pear Grove. It was a comforting sound, actually. It meant they hadn't given up on Margie yet. Maybe Doc had made it in time.

Sara noticed my change in posture and shook her head. "No, no—I didn't mean it. I'm just angry. Angry because my friend's gone, because my café is headed down the drain. It's easy to blame Margie for those things, but she didn't cause either one of them, not really. All she did was break up a good relationship."

My head was starting to hurt. I rubbed the bridge of my nose with the hope of getting rid of the headache before it really sunk its teeth in. "But they were already split up. I feel like I'm missing something."

Sara glanced out the front window as though checking whether someone might overhear her, and then lowered her voice. "Margie didn't tell you everything because she knew she'd get in trouble for it. I wouldn't tell you, either, except that Amelia's gone and Margie's gone, so it doesn't even matter anymore. When Margie said Cal and Amelia weren't happily married, she wasn't lying—not exactly. They *were* happy. Just not married."

I blinked. "Yes, they were. They had the same last name!"

"Nope. They lied about that. Margie found out through the pharmacy records. That's why she didn't tell you the whole story. She's an employee of the pharmacy, and if she was caught revealing private health information, the fines would put Doc out of business."

My jaw literally dropped. That explained why Cal couldn't get a copy of the ME's report—he wasn't *legally* Amelia's family. "But why did Cal and Amelia split up instead of just tying the knot? The waiting period is only a few days in Oregon. Heck, they could fly to Vegas and make their vows in an Elvis chapel in just a few hours."

"They couldn't. Amelia was already married to some English guy. He wouldn't agree to the divorce, and the separation period there is something like five years. She and Cal just couldn't wait. They wanted to be together—but pastors can't be shacking up with their girlfriends, you know?" Sara chuckled sadly.

I guessed at the end of the story. "So they moved from Idaho to Honeytree and lied to everyone here that they were already husband and wife until Amelia's divorce was granted and they could actually get married?"

Sara nodded.

"How do you know so much about Cal and Amelia's relationship?"

Sara stuck out her chin defensively. "If you must know, Amelia was staying on my couch. She didn't have anyone else to talk to, so I heard about everything. You know, Amelia *told* Cal not to run. She told him it would all come out."

"She was right about that. He finally realized it at the cocktail party, I think. That's why they got back together, because he agreed to drop out of the race."

Sara's eyes bugged.

"You didn't know? They spent Friday night after the cocktail party together. Cal planned to withdraw his candidacy on Easter Sunday."

"So that's why she didn't come home," Sara murmured, her gaze distant. "I thought it was something I—well, never mind."

"What could you possibly have done?"

Sarah's cheeks flushed again, and she stubbed her toe on the floor sheepishly. "Well, Margie and Doc are my landlords. I couldn't really take down the signs, could I?" She gestured to the *Morrow for Tomorrow* campaign sign taped in the front window. "But Amelia didn't understand that. She said I had to stand up for my principles instead of hiding behind my business. I called her a hypocrite. And as you can imagine, that didn't go over well. That was the last time I spoke to her. She avoided me at the cocktail party and then I never saw her again." She blinked away the tears that welled in her large, dark-fringed eyes.

"I'm sorry, Sara," I said quietly. I couldn't imagine how it felt to lose such a close friend. What if the last conversation I had with Ruth or Eli was our last conversation ever? With a jolt, I remembered where I'd left Eli—alone, desperately trying to revive Margie. Had he succeeded, or was he now feeling the sting of Margie's life slipping through his fingers? "I'd better go."

"I understand." Sara's face twisted. "I'm sorry you got wrapped up in everything—it's my fault."

"No, it's not," I assured her. "Not any more than it's Cal's or Doc's. We're all just victims of circumstance."

She offered me a grateful smile as she unlocked the front door to let me out. But as I walked toward City Hall, my feet felt heavier with every step. Had two women in Honeytree really been *accidentally* poisoned within a week of each other? Two women who just *happened* to be connected to a contentious mayoral election? Who *happened* to have eaten food served to them by Sara? Who *happened* to smooth the path for Cal's election? That didn't seem like a single fluke. That was a lot of flukes. A whole flock of flukes.

Chapter 17

I found Eli in his office, his head bent over a sheaf of paperwork. He glanced up only briefly when I walked in, and then went back to filling in the stack of forms. I stood there awkwardly, waiting for him to finish before I asked the question burning on my tongue, but my impatience got the better of me.

"Is she OK? I heard the ambulance siren. They don't turn it on unless the person is alive, right?"

"Right."

Relief washed over me. Margie was alive. Eli re-started her heart, and then Doc got there with the Epi-Pen in time. I sank into the chair across from Eli. "How are *you* doing?"

"Fine," he said absentmindedly. Then the office was silent except for the sound of his rollerball pen on the paper.

Fine? Really? I waited a few beats and then blurted out, "I'd be a mess if I were you. I mean, you took a risk that you'd be poisoned along with Margie, performed CPR, narrowly saved her life, and then you're *fine*? Unless you're a robot, I don't believe it."

Eli dropped his pen on the paper and let out a frustrated sigh. "Do you mind, Leona? I really need to finish these reports."

I blinked. He was definitely not fine. I stood up and went

around the desk to tug on his arm. "Come on. You need to take a break. Not a long break!" I added quickly when I saw a flash of protest in his eyes. "Just come outside and get some air. Take a walk with me. The paperwork can wait a little bit longer."

He twisted his head to look at the clock behind him for a long beat. Then he looked back at me. Then a familiar, mischievous smile spread slowly across his face. "Sure, I'll go out with you."

"Go *outside*, I said. Not go out." I made a face at him. He stood and pulled on his jacket, still grinning like an idiot. "Don't get ahead of yourself, mister."

He paused a moment. "Should I wear my hat? Is that appropriate for a date or is it too official-sheriff's-business?"

"It's not a date!" I yelped. "It's just a walk!"

"It could keep the rain off if it starts to drizzle," he mused, stroking his chin. "But on the other hand, the brim might get in the way if I tried to kiss you."

"Wear the hat." I crossed my arms over my chest, my ears burning as he watched me gleefully. Why did he love torturing me so much? "Please, wear the hat."

"As you wish." He winked and swiped his hat from a hook on the wall, tipping it smoothly onto his head.

I ignored the *Princess Bride* reference and hurried to the door before he could open it for me. "I regret any ounce of sympathy I may have felt for you five minutes ago," I said when we got outside and headed down the block, matching our strides.

"I don't. Best sympathy ever," he chortled, still smug that he'd conned me into a date. Well, the joke was on him. I'd managed to get him away from his pile of papers and smiling to boot, no small feat after his harrowing morning. As if on cue, my stomach growled.

133

His face lit up even more. "Lunch!" he declared, veering toward the Rx.

"It's closed," I reminded him, and he stopped in the middle of the street. "Anyway, I have purse cookies. Want one?" I scrounged in my bag for the cookies I'd stashed during Sunday's reception and held one out to him.

"It's not closed," he said, frowning at my cookie. "Margie picked up drinks there this morning. I saw takeout cups on the floor at the scene."

"Sarah brought those to her with the doughnut," I explained. I put the cookies back in my bag—I wasn't going to waste them on someone who didn't appreciate quality emergency snacks. "She went to ask Margie for some leniency on the rent. Then when Margie collapsed, Sara ran and got Doc."

"I wondered how he knew—I figured Margie managed to get off a text message or something," Eli said thoughtfully as he stared in the direction of the pharmacy. The colored awning was just visible, peeking out behind the bank and the lawyer's office. Then his eyes came into focus on my face. "What else did Sara tell you?"

"Some pretty shocking stuff, actually." My stomach growled again, twisting painfully.

Eli's eyes slipped down my torso to my stomach and back up, and I couldn't help blushing at his scrutiny. He waggled his eyebrows. "Let's get a table for two at the Greasy Spoon and you can tell me all about it."

I remembered my last awkward exit from the Greasy Spoon and winced.

"Not a fan? I know it might be a little down-home for someone who's used to Beverly Hills fine dining…"

"Oh, no—I like Ed's cooking," I said. I'd had enough shaved

fennel salad and raw scallop crudo to last a lifetime when I lived in LA's most expensive neighborhood. Part of what I loved about moving back home was the simple, delicious comfort food that was served on every table, restaurant or otherwise. Give me corned beef and apple pie until the day I die!

"Well, good!" As Eli spoke the words, a light sprinkle started up, and we quickened our pace for the last couple of blocks to beat the spring rain. But before we reached the little diner, the clouds opened up into a true downpour. Eli held one side of his jacket out over my head as we ran the final ten yards across the parking lot.

"See? I was right about the hat," I said smugly, as we arrived inside the restaurant slightly damp and more than slightly breathless. Jillian's face lit up when she saw us enter and she waved at us from across the room.

"I'll be right with you!" she called, then turned back to the table whose order she'd been taking. The diner was as packed as the last time I'd been inside, and the air vibrated with the clink of coffee cups, the low chatter of happy customers, the hiss of the flat top, and the smell of delicious, delicious bacon frying.

My mouth began to water, and I looked around for an empty table. The only open seats were at the counter. I shrugged at Eli and headed for it, sliding into my stool just as Ed turned around and slammed his hand down on the bell. "Order up! Table 9!"

Jillian reached around me to grab the plates and paused to ask, "Coffee?"

"You know it." Eli flipped the two mugs in front of us over.

"Decaf for me," I added. Jillian gave a pert nod and flitted off to deliver Table 9's meal.

Eli rolled his eyes at me. "Sacrilege. What's the point of coffee without the dose of good humor? It's just bitter, brown bean-water without it."

"If I have caffeine after noon, it keeps me up all night," I explained.

The corner of Eli's mouth quirked. "I wouldn't mind staying up with you."

Heat bloomed from my collarbone all the way up to my hairline. Motherclucker, I handed that one right to him. I wondered if he flirted with everyone like this. Probably. I cleared my throat and stared straight ahead as Jillian poured our coffee.

"What'll you two have? The burger special is smothered and covered." She twitched her ponytail over her shoulder and stared at us expectantly.

"I'll take two," Eli said. "No bun, no fries, please."

I looked at him in surprise. "You're on a diet?"

"Gotta keep it spicy if I'm going to catch your eye." He patted his already very toned abdomen, a stark contrast with my own soft stomach. I suddenly felt self-conscious and crossed my arms over my comfortable rolls.

Jillian giggled at Eli, reminding me that she was still there waiting for me to order. I cleared my throat and fanned myself with my napkin. "Um—a cheese omelet, please. Three eggs, bacon on the side. And toast—extra toast."

"Eggs, huh? You're brave." Jillian winked at me. "Nobody else has taken the plunge today."

Eli spun around on his stool, scanning the plates on the tables around us, and then snorted. "I changed my mind. Give me what she's having. I want eggs, too," he said loudly. The conversations around us paused as the other restaurant patrons

136

overheard, and then slowly the dull murmur returned, but this time with more glances darted our way.

Great. Just what I wanted—more attention. I knew Eli meant well, though. And maybe he was right. Maybe seeing the sheriff eat eggs would remind people that they were missing out on their favorite brunch food.

"You got it," Jillian said. "Two omelets, coming right up." She tacked up the order on the wheel and spun it around so Ed could grab it.

When she left, I leaned toward Eli. "You didn't have to do that. Change your order, I mean. You shouldn't sabotage your diet for me."

He blinked innocently. "I don't know what you're talking about. Cheese omelets fit my diet perfectly."

"And the extra toast?"

"I'll feed it to your chickens." He smiled crookedly at me. Darn it if that man didn't know the way to my heart was through my birds.

"Why are you so cute?" I asked, annoyed at my own reaction. He flirted with everyone, and I knew that, so why was I so susceptible? Old habits die hard, I guess.

"When you're the baby brother to seven sisters, you learn real quick how to bat those eyelashes." He demonstrated, his long eyelashes fluttering against his cheeks, and then grinned.

"Well, stop it. I can't concentrate when you do that." I rubbed my thumb on the countertop in a thin place where the black was showing through the white-with-gold-glitter Formica pattern.

To his credit, Eli didn't tease me any further. He was quiet a minute, and then said, apropos of nothing, "You promised to shock me. What did Sara tell you?"

137

Chapter 18

I lowered my voice so the local gossip mill wouldn't have any more grist. "Get this. Amelia and Cal weren't married." I raised my eyebrows, anticipating his reaction. But instead of shock, his face registered only mild interest.

"Right." He nodded. "That makes sense."

"No, it doesn't!" I yelped, then glanced around me to make sure I hadn't drawn attention from any of the people around us. I took a deep breath and continued in a milder tone, "It makes zero sense. *Everyone* thinks they're married."

"I meant it makes sense because it answers a question I had about the medical examiner's report when I saw the unredacted copy. It listed Amelia's last name as Brooks, not Goodbody."

"Why you didn't say anything?!"

Eli shrugged. "I figured that was her maiden name. A lot of women don't change it when they get married."

"I wish I hadn't," I muttered. My married name felt like a cattle brand: property of Peterson Davis, world-famous plastic surgeon, cruddy husband, and only slightly better father.

"So change it. You can use mine if you want. Leona Ramirez," Eli said, turning the words over on his tongue as he flapped those pretty eyelashes at me again.

"I told you not to do that eyelash thing," I reminded him. My

138

cheeks were burning so hot, I wanted to plunge my head in the pitcher of ice water that sat dripping on the end of counter. I sipped my decaf instead.

"So they weren't married. So what?" Eli prompted.

"So, Margie figured it out from pharmacy records and was using it against Cal. She threatened to tell everyone unless Cal dropped out of the race. And remember how Margie said that Cal was blackmailing *her*? I suspect that Cal threatened her in return—maybe he planned to turn her in for a HIPAA violation if she revealed their secret." Now that had to shock Eli. I was pleased to see his eyebrows raise slightly. The genius sheriff hadn't put *that* together yet.

Then to my disappointment, he shrugged. "That's politics. They were playing dirty, but I'm guessing that's typical. Personal attacks are part of the deal in most campaigns."

"How about poisonings? Are those part of the deal in most campaigns?"

Eli blinked at me. "I don't follow."

"Order up!" Ed said, sliding two large platters of food across the counter to us. He swiped our ticket off the spinner and dropped it into a trash can behind the counter. "Jilly'll bring your bread in a sec."

Approximately one second later, Jillian arrived with two small plates of toast and a wire rack filled with grape jelly packets. She whipped a bottle of hot sauce out of her apron pocket and set it down near Eli's elbow. "I know you like to keep it spicy," she said, and winked at him before bustling off with another order from Ed.

Eli laughed out loud as he unscrewed the top and shook hot sauce all over his plate. "Kid's got a real future in this business. You've got a good one, Ed." Ed looked over his shoulder and

139

grinned at Eli.

I dug into my plate. Even though it wasn't made with my eggs, the omelet was perfect. Thin, light, and fluffy, it was filled with sharp cheddar cheese and had a sprinkling of chives on top. I alternated between bites of the omelet and bites of the hot, buttered toast, savoring each mouthful. We were lucky to have two restaurants in town with food this good in a town as small as Honeytree.

I stopped mid-chew. Pretty soon, we'd only have one restaurant in town. The Rx Café was on its last legs. If Sara couldn't pay the rent, the restaurant was over. Closed.

I set down my fork and took a sip of my coffee. What could I possibly do to help her stay in business when I was barely staying in business myself?

Eli scooted his toast toward me. "You can have mine if you want. I noticed you ran out of toast before you ran out of eggs."

I looked down at my empty bread plate. "Oh. No. I'm full."

"Me, too." Eli raised his hand to get Jillian's attention and made the universal "bring the check" sign before turning back to me. "What's on your mind? You're not still thinking about Marge and Amelia, are you? I know it seems suspicious to have two accidents so close together, but it happens all the time in law enforcement. Especially in our area, where we don't see much crime. There'll be several car accidents in one week and then none for months."

"That's hardly random. Multiple car accidents could be due to weather conditions," I said, annoyed that he was interested in dismissing thoughts that I wasn't even having. But since he'd brought it up… "There are too many connections between Amelia and Marge. Both ate something served by Sara, right? Both keeled over within an hour…or minutes, in Marge's case. And both their deaths benefited Cal. That's too many coincidences."

"Marge isn't dead." Eli snatched a piece of toast from the plate he'd offered me and munched on the corner. Then, seeming to realize what he was doing, he put it down on his empty omelet plate.

"But she could have been. Whoever put the peanuts in the Boston cream doughnuts sure hoped so."

"Who'd do that, though?" Eli protested, leaning back as Jillian set the check on the counter between us. I swiped it before he could and handed Jillian my credit card. I held my right hand under the counter and crossed my fingers that the charge would clear.

"I don't know. That's your job, not mine. All I'm saying is that someone delivered poison right into Amelia and Margie's mouths." I signed the receipt that Jillian handed me and tucked the receipt into my purse. I started to pull out some cash for the tip, but Eli stopped me, putting a ten out of his own pocket on the counter.

Big tipper. He must have really liked that hot sauce.

Eli stood and plucked his hat off the stool next to him. "You're not suggesting Sara is going around poisoning people for no reason?"

A hush fell over the restaurant, and the omelet in my stomach suddenly turned to stone. I'd gotten too comfortable at the counter of the Greasy Spoon and forgotten that the ears of the town were trained on our conversation. "No," I said, and then again a little louder for the benefit of the peanut gallery, "No, definitely not."

"It was a fluke," Eli agreed, oblivious to the room. "An ugly coincidence."

I followed him outside, where the rain shower had vanished as quickly as it had begun. The sun peeked out from behind a bruise-black cloud, and a pale rainbow stretched across the bright blue sky from Cedar Street to the log pond. I'd have to drive right underneath its arch to get home.

By the time we got back to my car, it was gone, though.

"Want to keep me company while I finish my reports?" Eli asked. A surge of satisfaction came over me. That was the real Eli, the OK-Eli, not the tense and dismissive Eli I'd seen earlier.

"Can't. I need to get back to my flock." Our earlier conversation nagged at me, though. Sara *had* delivered the poison to Margie in that doughnut. That was a given. But Amelia was already sick when she got to the Rx Café on Saturday morning. "One thing—can I take a look at the ME's report on Amelia's death really quick?"

"Why?" Eli took off his hat and held it in front of him, and I hoped the move wasn't for kissing purposes. I walked a wide circle around him to the door of his office and waited impatiently for him to unlock it.

"I was just curious about something. I wondered what else Amelia had in her stomach on Saturday besides eggs."

"Oh, that's easy," Eli said. "I know that one off the top of my head. There were only two things: eggs and coffee. The perfect breakfast"—he nudged me playfully—"or lunch."

Bile rose in my throat. Coffee and eggs for Amelia. Coffee and doughnuts for Margie. It sure sounded like Sara had been the one to deliver them both. But what I didn't understand was *why*. Sure, Sara might have argued with Margie about the café rent. She was a desperate tenant, and Margie's personality could be reason enough to want her dead. But what did Sara have against Amelia? They were *friends*. Sara gained nothing by Amelia's death. In fact, she'd lost everything.

"Oh no," Eli said, shaking his head as he unlocked the front door. "No, no, no. I recognize the look on your face. Do *not* get involved in this, Leona. Just go home and feed your chickens. And don't forget to bring me that golden egg next time you come into town, please. I'm already skating on thin ice sneaking it into evidence for you, anyway."

I did my best impression of his innocent puppy eyes. "If no crimes were committed, the egg isn't evidence of anything except an Easter egg hunt, is it? So I don't need to turn it in. I can cash it in, instead! What do you have to say about that, Mister Sheriff?"

His mouth opened and closed like a fish, but nothing came out.

"That's what I thought," I said sweetly, and got into my car.

Chapter 19

B oots hopped around my feet, scratching the bathmat and pecking hopefully at my shoelaces as I rummaged through the dirty clothes for my cargo pants. I finally found them wadded at the bottom of the pile, crusty with creek mud and still slightly damp from my Scramble adventures.

Ugh. I really should do laundry more often. I hoped the egg and its contents weren't ruined by their stint in the bathroom hamper. Now, where was it? I felt the pants up and down each leg until I found it, a hard lump in the pocket on the right leg, and fished it out.

The golden shell seemed none the worse for wear, and it was still sealed with a clear plastic sticker around the seam. Hopefully the damp hadn't penetrated inside to the prize code. A thousand bucks would solve a lot of my problems, namely the problem of feeding eighty-odd chickens whose eggs were unsaleable.

Boots cocked her head and stared at the egg in my hand. I grinned at her and held it out so she could see it better. "Yes, I just laid this one. Do you like it? Wanna see what's inside?"

She hopped a few steps closer, muttering and clucking curiously as she craned her neck up toward the egg. Then a bra strap hanging out of the hamper caught her eye and she swiveled her head toward it, giving a sharp squawk of discovery and delight. She grabbed it and started yanking on it like it was a juicy earthworm. I waved the egg at her, but she'd completely lost interest in me.

I snorted. That's what I got for talking to birdbrains.

Well, lucky for Boots, the golden egg was going to feed her for a lot longer than one worm slash bra strap. Lucky for me, too. But for some reason instead of feeling happy about it, I felt something else. A squirmy little worm of guilt was crawling around in my stomach, and I didn't know why.

Sure, the circumstances under which I'd found the egg weren't great—I mean, it *was* in the hand of a dead woman—but I'd solved the riddle fair and square. I deserved the prize. So why did I feel bad about claiming it?

Maybe it was because I knew other people needed it more than I did. At least *my* house was paid off with my divorce settlement. I'd have a place to live even if my chicken operation failed. But Ruth had sabotaged her own real estate deal on my behalf, and she had payments on her shop *and* her house. Without some income, she might lose both.

Maybe I could split the prize with Ruth. She was my Scramble partner, after all. Five hundred bucks wouldn't solve her problems, just like it wouldn't solve mine, but it'd be a Band-Aid until we figured out our next moves. That made me feel a little bit better.

I was just about to crack open the golden egg when I had another thought that gave me pause. What if Eli was wrong, and the two poisonings weren't just flukes? What if the egg really *was* evidence from a crime scene—a *huge*, terrible crime, Amelia's murder? Then it'd look really clucking suspicious that the person who found her body and the last person to see

145

Margie un-poisoned were the same person who walked away with a thousand dollars in cash.

I probably *should* turn it in, just in case. But that would mean no money for Ruth. Could I just sit back and let her struggle when I could have helped her out?

I groaned, and Boots dropped the bra strap to give me an accusatory glare. I waved her back to her task. "Sorry, didn't mean to interrupt you with my personal crisis."

I left her in the bathroom and took the egg out to the kitchen. I looked around for a safe place to keep it, finally settling on the hen-shaped cookie jar where I stored my stash of emergency cash. It could stay there for a few more days while I decided what to do with it.

Turn it in? Or cash it out?

I drummed my fingers on the kitchen table. It'd be a whole lot easier to claim the prize if I knew that Amelia's death was truly accidental. But at this point, that was impossible to prove.

Or was it?

All I *really* needed to do was rule out all the people who might have caused her death. I counted them off on my fingers. Suspect number one: Cal. Amelia's death had removed Cal's major campaign liability—his fake marriage. He planned to withdraw from the mayoral race until she died, and then he was right back on the stump. If that wasn't suspicious, I didn't know what was.

Suspect number two: Sara. I hated to put her on the list, but she'd been close to Amelia in her final days. They may have had some bad blood between them that nobody knew about. Also, she'd served the breakfast that Amelia ate that morning—the only things in Amelia's stomach were coffee and eggs. That was a hard fact.

No, I reminded myself. It wasn't. Sara had served Amelia eggs, sure. But if Amelia was acting sick at the Rx Café, maybe she'd had the coffee before she got to the restaurant. If I could prove that Cal had made Amelia coffee at home, maybe Eli would believe that her death wasn't an accident. I grabbed my phone and called Sara's number, praying that she'd pick up.

"Hi Leona," came her small voice over the line.

"Did you serve Amelia coffee on Saturday?" I blurted out.

"No." Her answer was instant, automatic, which gave me pause. Did she really remember Amelia's order among the dozens of customers she must have had that morning?

"Are you sure? You're not confusing her with someone else?"

"I'm sure." Sara's voice strengthened. "Really sure, actually. She usually gets cappuccinos, so I offered her one, but she said no thanks. She'd said she'd had enough caffeine already and it had upset her stomach. All she had was the scrambled eggs, no toast, no potatoes."

"No decaf, either?" I asked.

"Nope. I don't serve decaf. I'm morally opposed." Sara gave an awkward giggle.

Her, too? What was with all the anti-decaf activists in this town? But hey, she'd just made my life a lot easier—now I knew for sure that Amelia's coffee was poisoned, and she didn't drink it at Sara's café. "Did she happen to say where she picked up the coffee?"

"No, why?" Sara's voice took on a troubled tone. "You don't think…?"

I sighed. "I do think that, actually. Or at least, I think it's possible."

"Well." She paused. I could tell she was struggling with whether she should tell me something. Finally she said, "I'm not accusing them of anything, but I know she met with Margie and Doc before breakfast. She and Cal were working really closely with them on the Easter Scramble. But I have no idea if they drank coffee at the meeting."

"Where did they meet?" I asked. The only other place in town with coffee was the Greasy Spoon. Or had they met somewhere else, like City Hall or even one of their homes?

"She didn't say."

"Hm. I'll have to ask around," I murmured, more to myself than to Sara.

"Don't tell Doc I'm the one who told you about the meeting, OK?" Her voice was thick with regret and cracked on the last part of the question. "He already hates me for what I did to Margie."

I clucked my tongue. "He doesn't hate you. How could he? They were his doughnuts, anyway."

Hm. Doc's own doughnuts had poisoned his wife. Had his coffee poisoned Amelia?

My thoughts were interrupted by a knock at the front door that nearly jarred me out of my seat. I said a quick goodbye to Sara and went to see who had knocked, checking out of habit on the way to make sure I was wearing pants. I didn't want some poor Jehovah's Witness or vacuum salesperson to get the surprise of their lives when I opened the door.

I opened the door with "no thanks" on my lips, but it was just Stef from the post office. Her tan sedan with a big USPS sticker on the driver's side door was parked in the driveway. Usually she put any mail into the mailbox out by the highway. If it wouldn't fit in the box, then she'd just leave it on the porch. So I was surprised to see her outside my door holding nothing more than a slim envelope and a clipboard.

She handed me the clipboard and pointed to a box at the bottom. "Sign here."

I dutifully scribbled my illegible signature and handed it back. In return, she presented me with a stiff, legal-size envelope with a return address in Salem. "Thanks?"

"Sure thing." She gave a quick nod. "Have a good one!" she said over her shoulder as she bounded down the steps on the way to the car. Oh, to have that kind of spring in my step still.

I looked down at the envelope in my hands—it was from the state and stamped "REGISTERED" across the front—and tore it open. I scanned the letter inside. It was my inspection appointment, set for Thursday afternoon. Case number 8010. Complaint: Inadequate space for housing laying hens.

I frowned and looked up at the coop across the driveway, where my flock was milling placidly, scratching and pecking at leftover grain they'd uncovered from the morning's feed. Alarm Clock stood proudly on a stump, overseeing his kingdom. My chicken palace was just that—a palace compared to most egg-laying operations that caged their birds. Though I didn't pasture my chickens every day, they had more than adequate space inside the run. Maybe ten times the space required by law. Whoever had filed this complaint had never been to my farm.

It was probably some meddling gossip who thought they were doing the town a favor by shutting down my farm, even temporarily. Well, the yolk was on them—I'd pass this inspection with flying colors.

Chapter 20

Thursday, Day 6

I spent the next forty-eight hours running around like a chicken with my head cut off, collecting eggs that were now piling up on my kitchen counters, ignoring the bills that needed to be paid by the end of the month, cleaning out the nest boxes, dodging Eli's phone calls, and sweeping the front porch. Though I knew I'd easily meet the state guidelines, it didn't hurt to spruce the place up a little before the inspection.

By the time the inspector showed up after lunch on Thursday in a white pickup truck, the flock was spread out under the blossoming apple trees, gorging on their fill of bright spring grasses and fat caterpillars. I was on the porch, sitting with a book and a mug of decaf, opinions be darned, the picture of idyllic farm life. Let anyone say my chickens had inadequate space, and I'd laugh in their face.

The inspector, a tall, gangly man wearing a dark green Department of Agriculture cap, got out of the truck and squinted at me, tapping the embroidered name on the breast of his bomber jacket. "Inspector Noble from the ODA. You Leona Davis?"

I put down my book and squinted back at him. "Yep. But my friends call me 'Case Eight-one-oh-one.'"

"Well, I guess you've seen the complaint. Show me what you got." He grinned, exposing the gap between his large, yellowed front teeth.

"You're looking at it." I nodded toward the orchard. Inspector Noble raised his eyebrows, his lips working as he counted the chickens and wrote something in a narrow notebook that he pulled from an inner jacket pocket. Then he turned and eyed the coop and barn.

"I'll need to take some measurements," he said. "Do some calculations."

I snorted. "Really? I would think you could tell from here."

"You're welcome to accompany me. Most farmers do." He walked briskly across the driveway toward the coop, clamping the notebook to his side with one elbow while he unclipped a laser measuring tape from his belt. I guess I wasn't most farmers, because I wasn't even a little bit anxious about his findings. He could measure my bra size while he was at it, and I wasn't going to worry about it.

"I'll be inside," I called. "Just knock if you need anything."

Of course I glued myself to the kitchen window to keep an eye on my birds—and an eye on Inspector Noble in case he screwed anything up during his inspection. He moved quickly and efficiently around the coop, taking careful measurements of everything, even the headroom in the nest boxes, and noting it in his little book. When he finished with the coop, he headed for the barn with a quick, almost furtive look over his shoulder at the house.

I rolled my eyes. He probably thought he'd find a bunch of spare layers stashed in there. While I did occasionally use the barn stalls for quarantine of sick chickens, none of them lived in there permanently, simply because it wasn't completely predator-proof. Barns always had little cracks, holes, and gaps that a determined critter could sneak through, especially antique barns like mine.

Sure enough, he didn't spend five minutes in there. He spent more time in his truck filling out forms. When he finally came and knocked on my door, I took my time answering it and then couldn't help smirking at him. "How are your calculations? Everything check out?"

He gave me a wink and a nod. "Looks A-OK. I'll just need your signature in a few places. Mind if I come in? I smell coffee."

Pausing a split-second to eye him up and down and assess his threat level, I decided I could take an uncaffeinated, hairless camel in a fight, then led him into the kitchen table and offered him a seat. "I've got a pot of decaf; that's all."

He made a face. "Never mind. I'll pick up some real coffee in town." He pushed his papers across the table toward me. "Sign the areas I've highlighted, and you're back in business."

I sank into the chair and bent my head over the papers, flicking through and groaning at the ten-plus signatures required.

"Tell me about it," Inspector Noble said good-naturedly. "My hand got a cramp."

"Can I find out who filed the original complaint?" I asked, already on page three. I pressed the pen to the paper and signed with a flourish.

"Nope, it's an anonymous process. Usually, anyway. In your case, the complaint was filed with the governor's office, not us, and then they passed it down. So technically the state of

Oregon made the complaint." He snickered, the air whistling through his front teeth as he exhaled.

I froze in my seat. "What does that mean?"

He waved his hand. "Ah, don't worry about it now. You're in good shape. Some rich guy probably got his panties in a twist about your rooster crowing and thought he could call on friends in high places to make it stop. But this is a right-to-farm state, so the only way they can get you is to claim you're breaking livestock regulations. Lucky for you, you aren't."

"Lucky me," I echoed. I didn't know any rich guys except my ex-husband. Well, I'd met Jam and Jelly—they clearly had money to burn. But I'd gotten the call from the ODA suspending my license before Jam and Jelly even viewed the old Sutherland place next door. They didn't file a complaint about my chickens.

But I did know "guys" who might have connections in state government...namely one, a certain mayor who favored tweed skirt suits and had threatened my business if I didn't spread her nasty rumors. Maybe Margie had flexed a political muscle to show me she meant business.

"These eggs for personal consumption?" Inspector Noble asked casually, motioning to the dozens of egg cartons stacked on the counter.

"Um..." A surge of panic welled in my chest. I could lose my handler's license again if he thought I was storing eggs improperly. "Yes, of course. My eggs for sale are in the fridge. In both fridges, actually."

"Well, I'm certainly glad to hear that." He pulled out his notebook and jotted something down, then raised his head and flashed his yellow teeth at me again before rising from his chair. "Good to meet you, Ms. Davis. I hope we never have to meet again."

#

"That woman is a total—"

"Witch," I finished Ruth's sentence.

"I can't believe she'd do something like that." Ruth shook her head disbelievingly as she flipped her salon's door sign around to CLOSED and lowered the blinds on the front window. "Calling the *governor* on you!"

I shrugged and sank into one of the dryer chairs. "You were the one who warned me that she could be dangerous."

Ruth took the seat next to me. "I didn't think she'd do something like this, though. A person who'd purposely ruin a local business has *no* right to lead this town. I never thought I'd say this, but I think I'm going to vote for the pastor."

"She had to know I'd pass inspection," I said. "It was just a warning. She was letting me know she *could* damage my business, not trying to *actually* damage it. Not much, anyway."

"Well, I think she's rotten to the core. You could have had a booth at the farmers market today if she hadn't orchestrated this nonsense. That's real money she stole out of your pocket, not just a warning! You know"—Ruth turned to me, eyes shining—"while Margie's still in the hospital, you should apply for a booth permit for next week!"

"There's a six-week waiting period before you can apply again if you're denied," I said, shrugging. "Maybe I will in June."

"She didn't even accept your application, did she? She just tore it up, so there's no record you submitted it. And she's still sick from the peanuts, so she won't even know!"

"Who's working at City Hall?" I asked. I was surprised City Hall was open at all, if Margie was still laid up. Honeytree had such a threadbare city budget that they didn't even have a City Hall receptionist—the mayor fulfilled both functions. Maybe they had a clueless city council member filling in.

"Last I heard, Doc was acting as interim. Tammy Jenson was in—I know you hate her, but she's one of my best customers and this month is tight—she told me. Doc's been asked to fill in until the election. If Margie wins, she'll be out of the hospital by then. If Cal wins, he'll take over from Doc."

I shook my head, confused. "*Doc Morrow*'s the mayor now?"

"What? It's not that weird. Isn't it a thing? Like, if a guy dies in office, his wife finishes out his term or whatever?"

I snorted. "I don't think so. That's why God made vice presidents."

"We don't have a vice mayor!" Ruth giggled, and shrugged. "I guess everybody trusts Doc to keep the ball rolling until the election. It's not far off, now. In any case, it can't hurt to reapply for the permit. What do you have to lose?"

"Another fifteen bucks?" I got up and went to the window, parting the blinds to stare across the street at City Hall. The building was dark except for Eli's office window. "Looks like he's closed for the day, anyway."

"But the pharmacy's open until six. Doc's gotta be there. Go see him about it," Ruth urged.

"I do have a lot of eggs piling up," I mused. The farmers market would be the perfect place to unload them. Plus, the conversation would be a good excuse to ask Doc about his meeting with Cal and Amelia about the Easter Scramble—a meeting that at some point, had turned deadly.

Chapter 21

The pharmacy had a long line—well, long for Honeytree. Five people stood in front of the counter, and nobody stood behind it waiting on the customers. In the pharmacy booth, Doc glanced up and then wiped sweat from his brow with his shoulder as he resumed counting pills into a bottle. He was clearly hustling to fill prescriptions, and I guessed he hadn't hired new counter help to replace Margie. I got in line, tapping my foot impatiently as I waited for the slow crawl toward the register.

To my great relief, Doc brought out five white prescription bags all at once. "Thanks for waiting," he said to all of us in line as he nervously fumbled them onto the counter before he picked up the first customer's bag. "Bear with me," he added as he entered the information into the cash register. "Margie usually does this part so I might screw it up a time or two."

The man in front of me chuckled politely. "Don't worry about it, Doc. We're just glad Margie's OK."

Doc shot him a grateful smile. "So am I, believe me. I can't even find my keys without her telling me where they are."

I believed it. She pretty much controlled everything about his life—even who he golfed with, from the sound of it. How could he stand that kind of treatment on a daily basis? They'd been married so long, maybe he was used to it. I moved one place up in line as Doc finished with the first customer and moved on to the next.

The customer whose prescription had been filled made a detour on the way out the door and stopped by the little table to swipe a Pastry Palace cookie from a tray Doc had out. It was the same place where he'd left the doughnuts on Tuesday—the ones filled with the one thing that his wife was deathly allergic to, peanuts. It wasn't like that doughnut was random. Even if Sara hadn't delivered it into her hands at City Hall, Margie likely would have eaten it anyway.

I looked back at the counter where Doc was still sweating and fumbling through the remaining prescriptions. Maybe bumbling old Doc wasn't so happy being a side character on Margie's missions. Maybe he preferred the mayor's seat, for once.

By the time I made it to the front of the line, I was fully convinced that Doc had tried to off his wife, and maybe Amelia, too, although I didn't know why. Maybe some huge power grab?

Doc looked surprised when I reached the front of the line and he didn't have any bags left on the counter. He spread out his hands helplessly, as if to demonstrate that he didn't have any pill bottles with my name on them hidden up his sleeve. "Are you sure your doctor called in the prescription?" he asked.

"I'm not sick. I'm here about Margie, actually." I narrowed my eyes at him. "And Amelia."

"Amelia Goodbody?" He blinked owlishly.

I nodded, leaning toward him over the counter. "You and Margie met with the Goodbodys on the morning of the Scramble, and then Amelia dropped dead. Then Margie very nearly dies. And why? Because you made sure she had one of those tainted Boston cream doughnuts. I mean, who would blame you for her peanut allergy kicking in? You put them out on the table over there, hoping she'd grab one for breakfast. But she didn't, so when Sara came by later in the morning, you saw an opportunity. Send *her* to Margie with a poison doughnut and throw suspicion even further from yourself!"

Doc took a step backward and smoothed his combover nervously, his lips trembling. "I don't know what you're talking about. I took Margie's Epi-Pen to her as fast as I could. She would have died without it. You saw me run out of here like a bat out of a belfry."

I thought back to that morning and remembered my surprise that Doc could move so quickly. He'd seemed very motivated to save Margie's life. Wouldn't he have dawdled if he wanted her dead? My certainty in my theory wavered. "Maybe you just wanted her sick—out of the way, not dead."

"That's not true. Margie's my everything—I'm a mess without her! She usually takes care of everything, and I can't even take care of myself." He leaned against the shelves behind him, jostling the boxes of decongestants and condoms and knocking several of them to the floor. He sighed heavily as he retrieved them and set them back on the now-untidy shelf, then struggled to straighten them, knocking against a display of lip glosses behind the counter. It fell backward, knocking down the rest of the identical boxes like dominos, and he rolled his eyes. "See what I mean? I can't wait for her to recover. I'm just"—his eyes moistened, and he rubbed away the tears roughly with his thumbs—"grateful. Grateful she's OK. It was touch-and-go for a while there."

I swallowed. If Doc was faking those tears, he should be in

the movies. Now I felt bad for accusing him of attempting to murder the wife he obviously loved very much. "I'm grateful, too," I said sheepishly. I never thought I'd be saying that about Margie Morrow, but here I was, thankful that the woman who'd sicced the ODA on my farm was healthy.

"It's funny you mentioned Amelia, though." Doc's forehead furrowed into a half-dozen wrinkles. "Because those doughnuts were from the church. Pastor Cal dropped them off, said they were left over from some campaign event they had up there. He was giving them out to businesses around town—I figured he was buttering up the Chamber of Commerce to vote for him. It was a bit surprising he stopped off here, though. Marge and I weren't on good terms with him."

"Imagine that," I said wryly. Blackmail would do that to you. Still, I wondered whether Cal was angry enough with Margie to tamper with the doughnuts before he dropped them off. Attempting murder is a pretty drastic reaction, even to blackmail. Unless that's not why he was angry... "Do you think there's a chance Cal blamed your wife for Amelia's death?"

Doc jerked his head up to stare at me. "Why in the world would he blame Margie?"

"Well"—I shifted uncomfortably as I tried to phrase things tactfully, which has never been my strong suit—"you did have a meeting with him that morning. Right before Amelia got sick."

"So? She was alive and well at the meeting." He pursed his lips at me, shook his head, and then ambled toward the table in the corner.

I followed him like a chicken hunting a mealworm. "So it's likely that she ingested the poison around that time."

"You want a cookie?" he asked me, his hand poised to pluck

159

one from the tray.

Now it was my turn to eye *him* warily. He didn't really think I'd eat anything he gave me after two women close to him were poisoned in the last week, did he? I shook my head. "Did you see Amelia eat or drink anything?"

Doc frowned, a large snickerdoodle halfway to his mouth, as he considered my question. "No, I don't think so. Well, there was coffee. I almost forgot."

My ears perked up and my heart began to beat faster. I tried to remember if I'd seen a coffee pot at City Hall. It didn't seem likely they had a pot in the office, since Sara had brought Margie coffee along with the doughnut. Someone had to have made it elsewhere and brought it to the meeting.

I tried to make my question sound casual. "Who lugged all the coffee to City Hall?"

"Nobody. The Scramble meeting was at the church," Doc said around a mouthful of cookie. "There was one of those big urns they use for receptions after service. Styrofoam cups in a stack. I don't know who brewed it—it was hot and ready before Marge and I got there, and we left before we got to drink ours."

"Did you see Amelia have some?"

Doc's face scrunched up as he tried to remember the morning. "Let's see. We were sitting around a table, with Cal and Preston across from us. I know they didn't have coffee. I remember they passed on it because Cal had some dental thing and Preston doesn't drink caffeine. Amelia was to my right. Did she have a cup in front of her? Yes!" he said triumphantly, pointing a finger into the air. "She did! She stood up from the table when all the shouting was going on and asked if anyone wanted a refill. I think she was hoping to defuse the tension.

But Margie and I were so busy arguing that we didn't need refills. We hadn't even taken a sip before we left." He took another bite of his cookie and chewed it thoughtfully, a few small crumbs escaping and sprinkling down the front of his shirt.

"Why was everyone so angry?"

Doc stopped chewing for a moment. Then he resumed at a more leisurely pace. When he finished the bite, he said lightly, "You know. This and that. People get worked up about all kinds of things."

I rolled my eyes. I really didn't have time to pretend I didn't know about things I knew about. "So it was about the whole blackmail situation?"

Doc dropped his cookie on the floor, his mouth agape. "You know about that?"

"I know Margie found out Cal and Amelia weren't married, and then used that to try and get Cal to drop out of the race."

Doc flushed and picked up his cookie, examining it closely to avoid looking me in the eye. I wondered if he was going to eat it despite the visible carpet fibers stuck to it. But to my great relief, he tossed it in the trash can and picked up a new cookie. "What else do you know?"

"I know she threatened to go public with the information, so Cal agreed to withdraw as a candidate."

"No, he didn't!" Crumbs sprayed from Doc's mouth as his face reddened. "I mean, we thought he did, but then he changed his mind, I guess. When Margie asked when Cal planned to announce that he was dropping out of the race, Preston blew up. He said if Margie whispered a word about Cal and Amelia, he'd turn us both in for violating state privacy laws. The fine for a HIPAA violation is a million bucks!"

"I take it you don't have a million bucks," I said sympathetically.

He snorted. "Hardly! If I did, I would hire someone to work the register. This place barely breaks even since Huge-Mart opened in Pear Grove. We need every cent of Margie's mayoral stipend to pay the bills. Why else do you think I agreed to be the acting mayor?"

"Limitless power?" I joked.

He snorted. "I find it repugnant, actually. But I'll hold my nose if it means my business stays afloat."

I felt a pang of sympathy for the Morrows. This whole debacle was stretching everyone's wallet thin. "I know the feeling. My eggs are piling up, and I can't sell them to Sara now that she's forced to close up shop."

The guilty expression that washed across Doc's face reminded me that he was the one evicting her. I'd forgotten for a moment that he was her landlord. He sighed heavily. "I want to throw her a lifeline, but I worry that she won't be able to pay next month, either. Might be better to look for a new tenant."

"Or...you could use your new mayoral powers for good and hire her to cater the election night bash." I raised my eyebrows suggestively. "Surely that would cover the rent for May."

Doc paused in the middle of reaching for another cookie, a rocky road one with marshmallows in the middle, this time. "Isn't that lining my own pockets with city funds? That hardly seems ethical."

I chuckled internally. Apparently, the old adage that opposites attract was true. I couldn't imagine those words—*that hardly seems ethical*—coming out of Margie's mouth. She'd do pretty much anything short of breaking the law. But it was comforting to hear that Doc had a little more of a conscience. "Call it a coincidence that the only local caterer also happens to be your tenant. Why hire someone who doesn't even live here? Keep Honeytree's money right here in town."

Doc squinted one eye as he considered what I'd said. Finally, he said slowly, "It's not a terrible thought. I'll consider it."

A smile spread across my face as I let out the breath I'd been holding. "Great! And while you're wearing your mayor hat, can you approve a permit for a farmers market booth? I have my egg handler's license right here." I pulled the folded piece of paper from my purse and held it out to him.

To my surprise, Doc shook his head vehemently as he stepped back from me, waving his hands to refuse my license. "Nope. Can't do it."

"Why not?" I protested, a lump rising in my throat.

Doc avoided making eye contact with me as he busily brushed the crumbs from his shirt front and adjusted his shirt cuffs. "I'm not approving any new permits—not until after the election. It's just not fair to Margie or Cal if I make that kind of decision without their input. It's not far off, so you'll just have to wait a couple more weeks."

I wanted to screech with frustration. I did some quick mental math. Two weeks of eggs piling up, and I'd have eighty or ninety dozen more! I couldn't store that many unless I had a restaurant-style walk-in refrigerator. I cast around desperately for a solution. The only point of hope was that Margie, stuck in her hospital bed, probably hadn't told Doc about rejecting my previous application.

"Surely Margie would approve me," I lied glibly. "What if Cal agreed as well? If he did, would you consider issuing me the permit? That way the election results don't matter."

"Oh, they matter!" Doc declared. Loyal to a fault, that guy.

"Of course—they matter. But they wouldn't be a factor in deciding whether to approve me for a farmers market booth. It's such a minor thing, not like a building permit or even a business license!" I attempted one of Eli's innocent blinking routines, hoping I looked more like a Girl Scout selling cookies than a menopausal chicken farmer with an eyeball affliction.

After another minute of consideration, Doc gave a grunt of approval. "If Cal agrees."

Nearly leaping out of my shoes, I flung my arms around his neck in a grateful hug. "Thanks, Doc! You won't regret it!"

Outside, no lights shone down the hill from the windows of the Church of the Everlasting, so I headed home for the evening, my stomach grumbling for dinner despite my big brunch earlier. I'd have to wait until tomorrow to speak with Cal. I almost stopped off for a burger at the Greasy Spoon, but the thought of all the eggs piled up on my counters tempted me home. I'd do my egg-farming duty and have an omelet for dinner, maybe with a little goat cheese and asparagus inside.

My stomach growled again at the thought of dinner, so I downed both purse cookies as I drove home. They were a tiny bit stale, but at least I knew they were safe. With all the women being poisoned in Honeytree lately, I wanted to know exactly what was in my food. I was ashamed of my own paranoia. I sounded like Tammy Jenson, I chastised myself as I drove home through the Curves, suspecting everyone based on zero evidence!

But there was *some* evidence backing up my suspicions.

My conversation with Doc had shed light on two important things. One, it was certain that Amelia had coffee at the church on Saturday and had probably ingested the tetrodotoxin there.

And two, the doughnuts that poisoned Margie with peanut oil were from the church, too.

Chapter 22

Friday, Day 7

After my morning chicken chores and an hour of egg-washing, sorting, and labeling, I changed into my good jeans—the ones without any rips or stains—and bid Boots goodbye. The sun was out, so I decided to wake my little red convertible from her safe, cozy spot in the barn and let her stretch her legs. The only vestige of my life in LA, the Porsche was the one thing I hadn't been able to give up from that lifestyle. I was looking forward to the dry Oregon summer when I'd be able to drive her more often, and I babied her like a souffle just out of the oven as I eased her out through the barn doors.

On the highway, I reveled in the feeling of the wind in my hair. I might show up in Pastor Cal's office looking like a lion who stuck her finger in a light socket, but man, it was worth it for these few blissful moments. I was in my element, and I was heading to get my farmers market booth approved. Everything was going to be OK. I eased off the gas when I hit the city limits, and it was like coming down to earth after a rocket trip to the moon.

When I pulled up to the church, I groaned. Eli's black SUV with "Sheriff" printed in gold letters on the side was already parked right in front. Suddenly my lion's mane didn't seem like such a good look. I grabbed a hair tie from the glove compartment and bundled my hair into some excuse for a bun using my reflection in the rearview. I couldn't see my whole head in the small slice of mirror, but it'd have to do. And at least I had on my good jeans.

The creak of the church doors echoed through the sanctuary as I pushed them open, bracing myself for a confrontation with Eli. He'd given me clear instructions to bring him the golden Scramble egg, and to *not* get involved in pursuing my suspicions about Amelia's death, and here I was flagrantly doing neither of the things he'd asked. Well, he could kiss my—

"Hey! What're you doing here?" Eli's voice boomed across the room. I nearly peed my pants a little. I hadn't spotted him leaning in the open doorway to Cal's office.

"Farmers market!" I squeaked. It wasn't a lie. It wasn't a lie. It wasn't a lie. I blinked rapidly as I hustled over to the office and brushed past him. "I came to talk to Cal about the farmers market."

Cal looked up in surprise from where he was seated at his desk, his face pale. Preston was lounging in one of the armchairs nearby but sat up instantly when he saw me.

"This is a private conversation," he snapped, rising to his feet. "Cal's not involved in organizing the farmers market, anyway."

"Doc said—" I began, but Preston cut me off.

"Doc doesn't know what he's talking about. He should really mind his own business." He took my elbow and gently but urgently ushered me back the way I'd come, past Eli into the sanctuary.

I dug in my heels and turned around, craning my neck to see Cal still at his desk. "It'll just take a minute!" I called.

"I'm pretty much done, anyway," Eli said mildly to Preston as we passed him. He added in a low voice for my benefit, "The county released Amelia for burial."

A heaviness settled on my heart. No wonder Preston was acting so protective of Cal. Cal had finally been given permission to bury his wife. "I'm sorry—I shouldn't have interrupted."

"No, no." Cal motioned me back in. I shot Preston and Eli an apologetic look and made my way to Cal's desk.

"I'd like to have a booth to sell my eggs at the farmers market next week," I explained quickly, feeling stupid for broaching such a lightweight subject when he was coping with such emotional circumstances. "Doc won't issue me a permit unless you also agree."

"Fine, I agree," Cal said, nodding. "I'll give Doc a call and let him know. I need to call him, anyway, to see if he'll perform Amelia's service."

I swallowed hard. "Thank you."

"I advise against it," Preston snapped, joining me at the desk. "You're making the decision off the cuff, Cal—there may be consequences that you can't anticipate until you're in the mayor's seat. You don't want to make a campaign promise that you can't keep once you're in office."

Cal's forehead creased with bewilderment. "It's a farmers market booth, not a tax levy. I hardly think I'll regret the decision."

"Hmph." Preston's face twisted sourly.

"It's fine if it's temporary," I assured Cal. "You can revoke it any time if you get elected."

"*When* he gets elected," Preston said firmly. "He's the only real choice on the ballot. I'm just saying that you may wish to balance the needs of other businesses in town. You don't want to put all your *eggs* in one basket. What if Ray"—he meant the owner of the grocery store—"objects to someone selling eggs across the street and pulls support from your campaign?"

"It's only one day a week. I'd like to think Ray is more reasonable than that." A hint of irritation crept into Cal's tone, and his expression grew sulky. "I think all Honeytree businesses are valuable, not just the biggest one!"

"Ray's is hardly the biggest! There's the sawmill, the RV factory, all the logging outfits—heck, Doc's pharmacy is probably up there." Preston went on a bender, naming all the businesses in town. He was wrong about a lot of them—Doc's for sure. From what Doc had said, his business was pretty small. "We need their financial support to do one last ad push this week if we're going to capitalize on the sympathy for Amelia!"

I gasped aloud. I couldn't help it. It seemed that Cal really was using his wife's death as a strategy to win the election. Of course, I'd heard it before. Margie had said the same thing, but I thought that was just part of her power-hungry delusions. But this time it was straight out of his campaign manager's mouth.

Cal's pale complexion reddened. "You should rephrase that," he said to Preston with a warning edge to his tone. He stood, and somehow the height difference between them grew. Cal practically towered over Preston. He looked angry—but whether because Preston had exposed him or offended him, I couldn't tell. All I knew was that Amelia's death and Margie's almost-death were pretty darn convenient for Cal. His illicit non-marriage to Amelia was no longer an issue now that she was dead, and the woman who knew his secret and was unethical enough to spread it around was silenced—at least temporarily.

"What about when Margie gets better?" I blurted out. "Even if you win, she might still talk—despite your attempts at blackmail."

Preston and Cal both turned to stare at me, and I quailed, shuffling backward until I bumped into Eli, who I'd forgotten was even there. I relaxed against him, relieved to have the sheriff literally standing behind me. Because it wasn't until that moment, with both of them looking at me with anger in their eyes, that I realized someone else knew Cal's secret—*I* did. And if this was a secret worth killing for, then maybe I was next in line.

"I don't know what you're talking about," Cal said, never taking his gaze off me.

"Drop it, Leona," Eli said through his teeth behind me, the way he'd say it to a dog who'd gotten ahold of something it shouldn't. Of course, I ignored him.

"At the Scramble meeting on Saturday—" I began. I broke off when pain flashed cross Cal's face, his forehead creased and eyelids crushed shut as he recalled that morning. But he couldn't use Amelia's death to manipulate me the way he was using it to manipulate the election. "You told Margie and Doc that you'd turn them in for a HIPAA violation if rumors about you and Amelia got out. You blackmailed them into silence for saying something *true*, all because you were so desperate to win the election."

"No, I didn't." Cal shook his head. "Amelia and I were going to pull out altogether. We just wanted to wait until Sunday to make the announcement, so we could tell our congregation first. That's all we were asking for—a little grace."

"You yelled at them!" I insisted, remembering Doc's version of events. "You bullied them right out of the room. Amelia jumped up to get coffee just to defuse the tension, remember? And that's the coffee that killed her."

"Leona—" Eli's voice warned behind me.

Cal stumbled backward, clutching the edge of his desk for balance. "No—that didn't happen. I was there. I never raised my voice, not once."

I couldn't believe he was lying outright. I put my hands on my hips. "Are you calling Doc Morrow a liar? He said there was so much screaming, he and Marge left the meeting!"

"It wasn't him. He didn't yell." Preston set his jaw, stepping between me and Cal. "It was me. He wasn't in the room. He stepped out for a moment."

Right. How convenient. I rolled my eyes.

"What?" Cal sank down in his seat. "I don't remember leaving the meeting except to..." His voice trailed off as realization dawned in his eyes and he ran his tongue over his teeth. "My whitening strips. I ducked into the bathroom to take them off. When I got back, Margie and Doc had left. I thought they were just eager to get going on their Scramble duties." He shook his head and glared at Preston. "You should have told me."

"I took care of the problem," Preston said calmly, smoothing the lapels of his crisp navy suit. He'd recovered his composure. "I didn't think it'd come up again."

"There was no problem to take care of, though!" I said hotly. "Cal and Amelia planned to quit the campaign. He had already decided that lying about their marriage wasn't worth it. What gave you the right to lay into the Morrows on his behalf?" I made eye contact with Cal, who was sitting there in his fancy pastor's chair looking paralyzed as he glanced between me and Preston. "Is this the kind of person you want working for you?"

Before Cal could answer, Preston snapped back at me. "That's enough! It's my job to insulate him from nonsense, and right now, that nonsense is you. Sheriff, will you please escort her out?"

My mouth fell open. Escorted out by the sheriff? Really? He couldn't just nicely ask me to leave? I turned and shook my head at Eli. "Oh, no. I don't need escorting."

Preston's lip curled. "I think you do."

"Just come on," Eli murmured in my ear and took my elbow.

I shot him an irritated look, but I grudgingly allowed him to guide me through the sanctuary toward the exit. "He could have just nicely asked me to leave."

Eli snorted as he held the front door open for me. "I doubt that would have worked. You were on a roll, and I know how you get when you're on a roll. You're like a lion running down an antelope."

I made a face at him. I really didn't appreciate the lion comment, given my hair situation.

"But listen"—he let the door fall shut—"I really think you should let this poor man have some peace. Whatever lies he told about his marriage, whatever ways he wronged Doc and Margie...even pastors make mistakes. He's paid the highest price for them, already. Badgering him about it won't solve anything."

"It might solve a murder," I muttered.

"For the last time, there was no murder!" Eli ran his hands

172

through his hair frustratedly. Now who looked like a lion? "Stop worrying about it. You should be worrying about yourself instead. You realize you blew your chances at that farmers market booth in there, right?"

To be honest, I'd kind of forgotten about the booth. "You don't think he'll call Doc for me?"

"Not after that performance!" Eli shook his head disbelievingly. "You need to chill out, wait until Cal is elected, and then appeal to him again. Apologize. Kiss his beatific buns. And then *maybe* you have a chance at gaining his approval."

Nausea swirled in my stomach at the thought of groveling at Pastor Cal's feet. I quit groveling a year ago when I walked out of my marriage. Thirty years of groveling for my ex-husband's approval were enough for me. And here was Eli, a man telling me to fluff another man's tailfeathers so I could *maybe* achieve my dreams? No way—if a man was standing in the way of my dreams, I was either mowing him down or dreaming up something even better.

"You're an idiot!" I snapped. "You're eating up Cal Goodbody's lies like a baby drinks milk. He's willing to do anything to win this election, and it's no coincidence that two powerful women have been taken down in the last week. Did you know that the peanut-poisoned doughnut Margie ate came from the church, too? Did you?"

By the look of his face, Eli didn't. I leaned in, my voice pitched high with emotion. "That man, the one you're treating like he already won the election, he gave a whole box of them to Doc. And Amelia *died* because she drank coffee here. You're letting a husband get away with the murder of his wife. You're letting a candidate get away with the attempted murder of his political rival. You're failing this *whole* town, Eli, because you don't want to make waves and lose your precious reputation with the powers-that-might-be. Well, I'm willing to lose it all. I'm willing to lose everything—my livelihood, my farm, even my friends. I'm definitely *not* going to put my head down low enough to get cheeky with Cal, as you so stupidly suggest."

Eli set his jaw, his eyes blazing so hot it almost seemed like sparks were flying out of them. "Leona—I don't think you mean that."

"Oh, I assure you, I do." I crossed my arms, daring him to contradict me. He wasn't the only one with fire inside. "And I'm going to let as many people know as I can."

"Fine, go tell Irene and Tammy all about it. Make your bed with the conspiracy theorists and gossips," he snapped. "See how far it gets you. But don't besmirch the sheriff's office because I refuse to play dirty. It's not a failure, it's a *choice*." He turned his back on me and walked away, headed to his SUV.

I wasn't done hollering at him, so I followed him to his car. "Don't walk away from me! You need a thicker skin if you're going to work with the public every day."

"You're not public. And you're already under my skin, Leona." He jerked open the driver's door. "You're always saying you need space, right? Well, here's some space."

Then he slammed the door in my face and drove away.

Chapter 23

I sped home in a haze of anger, barely enjoying the way the Porsche handled the Curves. Half of me was angry with Eli for being so *weak*. He couldn't even answer to me. He didn't have an excuse for his so-called *choice* to do nothing in the face of Cal's lies. He just walked away.

The other half of me was angry with myself for sabotaging pretty much everything in my life. I could have at least gotten the motherclucking farmers market permit before I accused people of heinous crimes. And I could have maybe not been quite so rude to Eli. I didn't regret speaking my mind, but I did regret a few of the words I'd chosen. Namely, "idiot" and "stupid." He was neither of those things. And he was probably never going to speak to me again.

At least I still had Ruth. If I had her friendship, that was enough.

By the time I hit the Flats my boiling anger had settled into a simmer and I was able to actually relax a little and appreciate the wide-open feel of the sky above the valley floor as my little car zipped along. I shook out my lion's mane to its full glory and basked in the midday sun.

The white for-sale placard swung in front of the blueberry farm and caught my eye as I drove by. I'd been there when

Ruth put it up last fall. I'd helped dig the post hole for it, so I knew it was the type with a slot on top where the for-sale notice could be swapped out for a "sale pending" and then a "sold." But it didn't say "pending" now. It still just said "for sale."

That was odd. Ruth usually put up a pending sign as soon as the ink was dry on the paperwork. Maybe Jam and Jelly's offer had fallen through. My heart sank as I drove up to my cottage and parked near the porch. My flock scrambled to watch me get out of the car, hoping I had treats for them, but I ignored them and sank down on the porch chair to call the salon.

"Do or Dye," Ruth answered.

"Why isn't there a pending sign up next door?" I demanded.

"No 'hi, how are you?'" Ruth sounded amused, but I wasn't.

"Did those Californians punk out on the deal? I swear, I'll hunt them down and force-feed them non-organic foods until they make good on their offer if you need me to."

She chuckled. "Not exactly." The way she said it made my Ruth-radar tingle.

"What do you mean, *not exactly*?" I asked, a dark suspicion roiling in my chest.

"I may have reminded them about the murder that happened there before they signed the paperwork," she said breezily, confirming my worst fears. I guess I wasn't the only one who self-sabotaged. "They decided to keep looking."

"You didn't! Why, Ruth?"

She sniffed primly. "Disclosure is required by law."

Disclosure was one thing. I was pretty sure harping on it was another. "You promised you'd make the sale. That was our deal!"

"You promised you'd get a farmers market permit," she said

176

archly. "Do you have one?"

"No—but you didn't know that when you made sure Jam and Jelly would walk away from the deal."

Ruth snickered and a growl escaped my throat. "Sorry. Those nicknames still make me giggle."

"Be serious! How are you going to pay your mortgages this month without the sale?"

The smile left her voice. "I'll figure it out. I always do. I have my fingers crossed that something will pop on the market in the next twenty-four hours so I can show them before they head back home."

"That's your plan? Cross your fingers and hope?" I stood up and paced up and down the porch, panic screaming through my veins.

"Do you have a better one?" she asked, stopping me in my tracks.

I didn't. In fact, "cross my fingers and hope" was pretty much my plan at this point, too. What was I thinking? If anyone was a stupid idiot in the town of Honeytree, it was me. "Are they staying at the Stagecoach?" I named the only motel in Honeytree.

"No, Ermengarde's B&B in Duma," Ruth said absentmindedly. "You're not going to—"

I hung up on her and dashed for the driveway. I glanced between my Porsche and the Suburban for only a split-second before I chose the little convertible. I needed the speed. With only a ten- or fifteen-minute head start, I needed every spare second to convince Jam and Jelly to put in an offer before Ruth showed up to kill the deal.

I might sabotage my own life, but I'd be fully plucked before I'd let Ruth sabotage hers. I gripped the wheel so tight my knuckles turned white and floored it all the way to Duma.

Lucky me, Jam and Jelly were enjoying the porch rockers on Ermengarde's pink Queen Anne when I pulled up. Good, I didn't have to waste any time on small talk.

"Hey," I called to them as I jumped out of the car, waving an arm over my head and starting to jog toward them. "Good to see you!"

Jam lifted his wine glass toward me and pushed back a lock of hair that had flopped over his left eye. "It's the chicken lady!"

"We were just finishing lunch," Jelly added. She motioned with her own half-full glass to the empty rocker next to her, sloshing a little bit of the rosé onto the floorboards. "Join us?"

I pulled the chair around to face them instead of the view. "Listen. I've been thinking more about your winery plans. I want you to know—I'm in. The whole community dynamic thing? I'm down with it."

Jam's smile froze, and he shot a panicked look at Jelly. She gave a slight shake of her head, and he grimaced apologetically at me. "We're really looking for a property that already has established vines. We don't want to wait five years for grapes."

"You don't have to!"

"We know, we could buy them. But we'd rather use our own," Kelly said nicely. The kind of nice that means *get the cluck off this porch because you're ruining our view.*

This is for Ruth, I reminded myself. I took a deep breath and launched into the pitch I'd practiced in the car. "Now, I know this sounds crazy, but have you heard the saying that the best time to plant blueberries is five years ago?"

"We're in the wine business," Jam said, also very nicely.

Not yet, I thought but didn't say. "What I mean is, the blueberry farm has established bushes. They're the most productive in the valley. Only a crazy person would rip them out and start all over."

Jelly wasn't even pretending to be nice anymore. She straight-up rolled her eyes at me and spoke like I was a toddler who'd crayoned the cabinets. "That's why we're buying *elsewhere*. Because we want *grapes* to make *wine*."

"You don't need grapes," I said. "Not right away. Plant your vines on the hill above the house instead of taking out the berry bushes. You can make blueberry wine while you're waiting for your grape vines to mature. And apple wine with my apples. Fruit wine is a specialty product. Nobody else is doing it here—not yet, anyway. And you can buy the farm for a song. I know for a fact that you could offer a lot less than the asking price and still get it."

Jam and Jelly shared a skeptical look. But then I saw it—Jelly fluttered her eyelashes at Jam. Classic Eli Ramirez move. I knew in that moment that Jelly was on board.

"We know what happened there," Jam said to me, frowning.

"So what? Why should you give up on your dream because of someone else's tragedy?" I crossed my arms and leaned back in my chair. "That place is perfect. It's better than perfect. I know, because I live there."

"Sammy-wammy." Jelly put her hand on Jam's arm. "This really could be something."

Jam put his hand on top of hers, and I knew it was all over. "Is this what you want? Really?"

She beamed up at him, nodding. "Really really."

"Well, then I'll call Ruth! We'll put in an offer tonight!" Jam reached for his phone. I stood and moved toward the stairs to give them some privacy while they made the call. Ruth didn't answer, of course—she was in the middle of driving over here right now—but Jam left her a voicemail that I knew she'd be obligated to answer. It was her fiduciary duty to her client.

Well, that was that. I took a deep cleansing breath, as Ruth might say. My chickens would have to go. But the silver lining was that I'd be able to sell my apples to the winery next door. I said goodbye to the Californians, but before I could even descend the porch steps, Ruth tore up the street, squealing to a stop in front of the B&B.

Jam blinked. "That was fast."

"She's as excited as we are!" Jelly bounced on the balls of her feet and grinned at him.

Ruth didn't look excited when she got out of the car. She bore down on me with the expression a tornado might have when it faced down a trailer park. She intended to destroy me.

"They're ready to make an offer!" I said brightly when she neared, backing up slightly to avoid the bulk of her wrath.

She pulled up short. "You didn't!"

"I sure did!"

Ruth took in the two beaming faces behind me and pasted on a grudging smile. "Great," she said between her teeth. "Perfect. Leona, help me get the paperwork from the car?"

"I don't think you need—" I began, but she grabbed my wrist and hauled me down the steps to where she'd parked before I could finish the thought.

"I can't believe you," she said furiously under her breath as she rummaged through her trunk. "You don't really want these lunatics as neighbors, do you?"

"They have some good ideas. And you need the cash. This deal will pay your mortgage for a *year*. You can't afford to ruin it."

Ruth snorted. "They'll put you out of business. You can't

afford that, either."

"I'm already out of the egg business, in case you haven't noticed," I snapped. "I need to pivot, like Jam said. This helps us both, Ruth. Really. Trust me."

"Sorry. I don't buy it." She pulled a fat expandable file out of the trunk, checked the contents, then jammed it into her purple purse and stormed back toward the B&B porch with me tagging on her heels. At the bottom of the steps, she stopped so short that I bumped into her bag. "Go home, Leona! You've done enough."

"I want to make sure you don't need help with the paper-work," I said. Innocent eyelash flutter.

Ruth didn't fall for it, though. She just glared at me. Maybe the flutter only worked on men. "I've got it under control. You can go home now."

I smiled sweetly at her. "Don't forget, you have to present the offer to your client. It's the law."

Chapter 24

Saturday, Day 8

Alarm Clock's crow woke me the next morning. My favorite sound. Unfortunately, it was also a glaring reminder of what I'd set in motion—the end of my egg farm dreams. I groaned and rolled over in bed, pressing my face into the warm pillow.

Don't be negative, I chastised myself. I flipped over and stared at the cracks in the ceiling with the sheets still pulled up to my chin. This was the end of one dream, sure, but maybe the beginning of another. Selling eggs, selling apples, what was the difference, when it came down to it? Apple trees ate a lot less than chickens did, so my overhead would be lower.

Plus, I'd have so much more free time now that I didn't have any friends.

I forced myself to get out of bed and let Boots out of the downstairs bathroom. Then, with her clucking contentedly around my ankles, I made breakfast (scrambled eggs, of course) and coffee.

When I sat down at the table, Boots jumped up in my lap. At least I still had my house chicken. I could keep her, even if I had to get rid of the rest of them.

Outside, Alarm Clock's crow pealed again, and my throat tightened. I was going to miss that kid. Well, I was sure he'd find a good home at the livestock auction. The handful of young cockerels I'd gotten as "packing peanuts" in my hatchery order might find their way to a stewpot, but a beautiful, good-tempered rooster like Alarm Clock would likely find a good home, especially if I grouped him with some laying hens. I just needed to do a health check on each bird and then figure out a way to transport them all to the auction house in Roseburg.

"Guess I have my work cut out for me!" I said brightly to Boots, stroking her smooth feathers under the table. She muttered contentedly. "Will you be very sad to be an only chicken?"

She would, I realized. When she was a baby with crooked toes and splayed legs, she'd toddled joyfully after her nestmates, though she couldn't quite keep up. Even now that she was a house chicken and slept inside, she enjoyed roaming with the rest of the flock during the day. I hated to take that away from her.

"We'll keep a few friends," I assured her. Surely Jam and Jelly wouldn't mind if I had a small flock for my own personal eggs. I could build a smaller coop on the other side of the house so it wasn't visible from their place.

Boots clucked indignantly when I evicted her from my lap, swigged the rest of my coffee, and went out to do chores. The chickens milled around me as I topped off their feeder, scrubbed out and refilled their waterer, and distributed treats around the run for them to find later when they were scratching around.

How was I going to choose between them? I had to keep

Boots, of course, and probably Dr. Speckle, the feisty hen I'd inherited when I bought the place. I didn't know her age or how long she'd keep laying, so it didn't feel right passing her on if she was just going to end up as Sunday night dinner. I searched for her and picked her up for a cuddle.

Dr. Speckle tolerated my fawning for a few minutes and then stretched her neck enviously toward the ground where Alarm Clock was making a big show over some treats so the girls would come over and eat them. I released her with a sigh, and she hightailed it over to join the Magdas, the three hens I was keeping for a friend until she returned from helping her family through a health crisis. They blended right into my flock now that my pullets were full-grown, but I'd put hot-pink zip ties on their left legs so I could tell them apart from the others.

Obviously, I'd be keeping those three, although not permanently. Who else? I scanned the chicken run, my eyes blurring with tears until the chickens became one vaguely orange mass. Well, I didn't have to choose right this minute. I stumbled out, doing my best not to step on any bird toes and leaving the door open so they could wander the yard for a bit. As I watched from the porch, they spread out under the apple trees, scratching and hunting bugs, oblivious to the fact that their lives were about to be turned upside down.

Some would go to other farms like mine. Some to backyards in town. Some to a lifetime in a cage. Some to a certain death.

Their fates were unknown. A roll of the dice.

I felt like such a failure. I'd never have taken on all of these birds if I thought for a moment that I wouldn't care for them for their whole lives. The whole point of buying this farm was to live my authentic life, and here I was bailing on it after less than a year!

Boots clucked sympathetically beside me and jumped up onto my lap. As she nestled down, fluffing her feathers as though she was taking a dust bath on my admittedly dirty jeans, I realized I couldn't do it. I couldn't let them all go. Their fates *weren't* unknown, because I knew for a fact that they'd never have a better life anywhere else.

I pulled Boots to my chest and hugged her gently. "Hen of my heart, I have to do what's right. And what's right is keeping our not-so-little flock together." Boots wheezed slightly in response, and I realized I might be snuggling the little bird a bit too hard. I released her right away and she shot me a dirty look before she hopped down and rejoined the flock.

Now I just had to figure out how to break the news to Jam and Jelly that I wasn't going to liquidate my egg business and tear down my chicken palace.

But did I say I would? I implied it, but I didn't *promise* anything. I just said I was on board with their ideas. That could mean anything. Their assumptions were on them.

But...

Was it *right* to let them buy the property thinking that I meant one thing, when I planned to do another? Was I living my authentic life if I let them invest while believing in a misunderstanding?

I groaned.

This dilemma called for another cup of coffee—and definitely *not* decaf. I went inside and made a second cup of pour-over, relishing the warmth that seeped through the mug to my fingertips. When something feels right, it feels right.

My body stilled at the same time that my heart sped up.

That was the answer. I knew what was right and wrong in my heart. It was right to keep my flock. It was right to protect

185

Ruth's livelihood.

And I knew what was wrong, too.

It was wrong of Jam and Jelly to ask me to give up my dream—and so many lives, even if they were bird lives—when they didn't even know whether it would affect their winery plans. We'd work together once they closed on the place and began their operation. I could plant trees behind the coop to shield their view, if need be. We'd figure it out.

That felt right.

But as I sipped my coffee, I realized something else felt wrong. Something else was *off*.

Amelia's death.

It was a simple cup of coffee like this one, a warm drink designed to defuse an ugly argument, that had poisoned her. I knew in my heart that it wasn't an accident the poison ended up in her cup. Someone intended for her to die. And, I realized suddenly, I also knew who had done it.

I didn't know how to prove it, but I had an obligation to try.

I fished the golden prize egg out of the cookie jar on the kitchen windowsill and tucked it safely into my pocket so it wouldn't get lost while I wrangled the chickens back into their run. They weren't going to be happy about their free-range time being cut short today, but I needed to get into town.

I had evidence to turn in to the sheriff's office.

A handful of treats persuaded most of the flock to return to the coop. Boots flew up onto the porch post to escape the stampede. Once most of them were back in the run, I ran around like a crazy person, bent at the waist to avoid smacking my head on the bottom branches of the apple trees, rounding up the few who couldn't be bribed—including Dr. Speckle and a couple of the young cockerels.

When they were finally locked up safely and Boots had her treats in the bathroom, I took a few minutes to put on a clean shirt and twist my frizzed hair into ringlets, mimicking what Ruth had done for me earlier in the week. I wasn't trying to look good for Eli; I was just trying to look less crazy, so when I presented my crazy theory to him along with the egg, he didn't totally write me off.

"So the coffee made me realize..." I started, practicing my speech to my reflection in the mirror. No, that sounded too crazy.

I started again. "So the chickens made me realize..." No, that was even crazier. Well, I'd figure it out on the drive into town. I always did my best thinking in the car, anyway.

Chapter 25

As I blew down the Flats, I saw that the "sale pending" tag had been added to the for-sale sign in front of the blueberry farm. Ruth's seller must have accepted Jam and Jelly's offer last night. I was worried their bid might come in too low, but I guess it was impossible to resist cash in a rural market like this.

I hope it meant a big fat commission check for Ruth, too. I felt comforted, thinking that she was set up for a while. The sale meant I was in for some tough negotiations with those two, but I was ready. I could handle it.

Who I wasn't sure I could handle was Eli. I parked, rolling the golden egg around in my palm as I walked from my car to his office. I half-hoped he wasn't working so I could just drop the egg through the mail slot and run away. But he was probably there, even if he had the day off. That's just who he was.

I was right. He was so absorbed in filling out yet more paperwork that he didn't look up until I set the golden egg down on the desk in front of him and braced myself for a scolding.

He reached for it, eyebrows raised. "I thought you weren't turning this in."

"I changed my mind." I plopped down in the chair across the desk from him. "I don't want the money."

He rolled the egg on the desk in front of him, catching it with his other hand, then held it up. "You sure?"

I nodded and took a deep breath. "I'm sure. One condition, though…"

"Uh oh." Eli leaned back in his chair. "I'm a little afraid, now."

"Two conditions, actually. One, you accept my apology for calling you a stupid idiot." I smiled hopefully at him.

He snorted. "I would, but you haven't apologized yet."

He was really going to make me work for it. I guess he had every right to a full and sincere apology, and I *did* feel bad about it, so it wouldn't kill me. "You're right. I'm sorry for yelling at you. Really. I don't think you're stupid or an idiot. You're very smart and thoughtful." I flushed, barely able to look him in the eye.

"Go on." He made an encouraging motion, his eyes twinkling mischievously. "Tell me more about how wonderful I am."

I rolled my eyes. I wasn't *that* sorry. "Condition two, you have to hear me out about Amelia's murder." He started to protest, but I held up my hand. "Really. Please. Just listen to me. You don't have to do anything about it, but I have to tell you who killed her and why. The same person poisoned Margie with peanuts, I'm sure of it. I can't just stand by without saying something, or it'll never feel right in my heart. That's why I brought you the prize egg as evidence today, because I *know* the poisonings weren't accidental. I may not be able to arrest someone like you can, but at the very least, I can say something."

Eli's face grew solemn and his hands, which had been rolling the egg back and forth as I talked, stilled as he leaned toward

189

me over the desk. "OK, I'm listening."

He sat quietly as I laid out all the details as I understood them, attentive to every word, nodding as I explained each step on the path of my logic.

"But I can't prove any of it," I finished.

"Hm." He licked his lower lip as he processed what I'd told him. "You're right—there's no concrete evidence."

My heart sank. I guess some part of me was hoping he had some magic sheriff tricks that would somehow transform my theory into a plan of action.

"But I have to say…it makes perfect sense. It's the only explanation that fits," he continued. He plucked an evidence bag from a desk drawer and slid the golden egg inside.

"You believe me!"

"One hundred percent." But the pained look on his face told me everything I needed to know.

"I get it. That's not enough," I said simply.

"At this point, the only way I can arrest him is if he confesses. And I don't see him doing that. Not now that he's so close to what he wants. But I'll put this egg into evidence, and who knows. Maybe some other piece of evidence will appear that will allow us to open the case again. And in the meantime, I'll keep a close eye on our friendly neighborhood murderer."

"That could take years." I sighed. The election was less than two weeks away. The bad guy was probably relaxing now that I wasn't standing there in the church, less worried that he'd be exposed, much like a predator after a kill.

I remembered one night when I was a little girl. An animal had been terrorizing my dad's coop. He set a trap baited with a mother hen and her chicks and then sat there in the dark, waiting, until the predator, a raccoon, came back for more.

When the raccoon realized it was trapped and unable to reach the chickens, it erupted into a snarling tornado of fur and teeth. I hoped Amelia's killer would do the same.

"You know, when a predator kills your chickens, the best way to catch it is to bait the trap with chickens."

"What are you saying?" Eli rubbed his stubbled jaw, one eyebrow raised skeptically.

"I'm saying…give the killer what he wants, and he might let down his guard. Then at the last moment, we yank that prize away. He's more likely to crack if he thinks he's not going to get what he wants *right* at the moment that it's finally within his reach."

"I've seen crazier ideas work. Do you have a plan?"

I laid out my idea for him. "But it's risky," I finished worriedly. "What if he doesn't take the bait?"

"Then I'll just keep on his tail until he slips up," Eli said doggedly. "Now, if you'll excuse me, I'm going to go see Mayor Doc about the security for a certain upcoming city event."

I smiled. "And I'll go visit the church to plant some seeds. We'll see what blooms on election night. But before that, there's someone else I need to go see." My eyes slid past Eli to the window, where Ruth's salon was visible across the street.

"I'll walk you over and say 'hi,'" Eli said, offering his arm. I looped my elbow in his. I wasn't surprised that he wanted to come, too. If Eli flirted with Ruth as much as he flirted with me, it was no wonder they'd gotten close lately. He added, "But don't tell her about your plan, OK? The fewer people know about it, the better. At least until after the election."

I gave a quick nod as we crossed the street. I didn't want to keep secrets from Ruth, but I also knew that the chances the plan would work at all were slim—and if word got out

191

about what we had planned, Eli and I would both be tarred and feathered. "Agreed."

The bells jangled above the door as we entered the salon. To my surprise, Tambra was seated at her manicurist station. She looked tanned and rested from her Spring Break travels in a tropical-print halter top that showed off her freckled shoulders. She smiled widely when she saw us, her lipstick a perfect match to the hibiscus blossoms on her shirt. "Have you told her yet?"

She inclined her head slightly toward me, and I realized her question was for Eli. He shook his head and held a finger to his lips. "Not yet."

Ruth bustled over from the sinks, waving wet hands at Tambra. "Hush! Don't jinx us."

"What's going on?" I asked, frowning. I wasn't the only one keeping secrets.

"Nothing," Eli and Ruth chimed together. They shared a look and then burst into giggles.

My cheeks grew hot. They must think I was really stupid if they thought I hadn't noticed how much time they'd been spending together lately. Why didn't they just admit that they were in a relationship? I'm an adult; I can handle it when my friends become a couple, even if one of those friends is an ex. Or at least, I can pretend to handle it. They were two of my favorite people and both of them deserved to find happiness.

"I was just dropping off Leona," Eli said breezily, dropping my arm. "See you later, ladies."

Thank goodness he left. I was about to die of awkwardness. I hoped they'd admit they were dating sooner rather than later, so I didn't have to pretend I didn't know what was going on. After he'd passed the window outside, headed for the pharmacy, Ruth squinted at me. "Why'd you come in? Nails? I know it's not your hair. Your hair looks great." She reached around Tambra and tweaked a couple of my curls.

"I'm ready for you." Tambra picked up my favorite color, a golden orange that matched most of my laying hens but was actually named something like "perfect peach," and waved it at me.

I shook my head as I tried to shake off my humiliation. "I mean, I probably do need my nails done, but I came to apologize for yesterday."

"For what?" Ruth sounded genuinely curious. Tambra averted her eyes, seeming embarrassed to be seated between us literally in the middle of the conversation.

"I shouldn't have stuck my nose into the blueberry farm deal. I apologize for going behind your back and speaking with Jam and Jelly. I just couldn't let you sabotage your business, not on my behalf. I'll put up with them. I hope you'll forgive me now that it's all worked out." Then I held my breath, waiting for her reply.

I didn't have to wait long. Ruth sidestepped Tambra's manicurist station and enveloped me up in a big hug. "You don't need my forgiveness. It's fine."

"Aww," Tambra cooed. She stood up and put her arms around us both and squeezed. "I gotta get in on this for a minute. I missed you guys."

With Tambra's hand comfortingly on my shoulder and my face pressed into Ruth's cucumber-melon-scented hair, I murmured, "So...are you going to let me in on your little secret with Eli yet?"

Tambra dropped her arms, and Ruth pulled back to look at me briefly. Then she shook her head. "It's still too early. I'll let you know when things are more certain, I promise."

"OK," I said, taking a deep breath and letting it out again. "Whenever you're ready, I'm ready."

Chapter 26

Tuesday, Day 20

My stomach was in knots as I arranged deviled eggs on the huge trays in the community center kitchen. Sara, who Doc had hired to cater the election reception, scanned them over my shoulder.

"Those look great. I think you can squeeze a few more in, though. Remember, when people start eating, the platters empty out right away, so it's OK if they're a bit crowded to start. Oh, and don't forget the chives." She scooted a container of chopped herbs toward me on the counter.

"Right, the chives." I bent my head over my work, my heart thudding in my chest. In a few more minutes, the special election results would be announced and the mayor—new or old—would be sworn in. That was my go-time.

I snuck a peek out into the main room. It was packed with Honeytree citizens who were all eager to eat the free food—and learn who won the election, of course. But the free food was definitely the big draw. I hoped they liked eggs, because deviled eggs were the star of the show. And Sara's recipe was dynamite.

I was lucky that Sara got the catering contract. She'd ordered almost all of my backlog of eggs. Almost. The rest I'd been hauling around in a cooler in the back of my Suburban, yelling out my car window at anyone I could find. Surprisingly, it wasn't a terrible sales tactic. A few people even dropped by the farm to pick up more eggs once their first dozen ran out. Even without a farmers market booth, word of mouth was spreading that my eggs were more delicious than any grocery-store versions, with brighter yolks and firmer whites. I couldn't take credit, though—all the credit went to the spring grass and the orchard bugs.

I spotted Eli over by the exit, chatting with Ruth and Margie. Ruth had on her normal witchy-hippie gear, but Margie wore a turquoise taffeta cocktail dress with a white jacket and gloves. Her coronation gown, I supposed. She looked a little paler than usual, whether from her near-death experience or just a couple of weeks cooped up in the hospital, but her smile was bright as she fawned over Eli while Ruth giggled next to her.

Everybody fawned over Eli, it seemed. Good for him. Good for Ruth, too. He really was a catch.

I felt a tiny pang of regret that I hadn't realized that forty years ago, back when I took him to the Sadie Hawkins dance held right here in the community center. How different my life would have been if I'd stayed in Honeytree with him instead of running off to the big city as soon as I could and marrying someone else. I didn't regret my daughter or my grandchildren that resulted from my marriage to Peterson, but I wasted a lot of time living a life that wasn't mine.

Luckily, Ruth was smarter than I was.

"I think we can put the food out now," Sara announced. The Friends of the Library ladies and I each swooped up trays to carry out to the long banquet tables that had been set up along the back of the room, opposite the stage. Most of the crowd watched us like vultures, ready to descend as soon as we set down the finger food.

Preston nabbed a deviled egg from my tray as I passed him and popped it in his mouth, waggling his eyebrows at me. He reached for another one, but I batted his hand away. "Mind your manners!" I said, keeping my tone light.

"It's for him!" he protested around the mouthful. He jerked his thumb toward Cal, who stood next to him in a tailored, charcoal-gray suit. He had that shiny, freshly shaved look, and his jaw was working as he tensed and relaxed it, staring at the blue box on stage that held the election results. Saying he looked nervous was the understatement of the century. He looked like he was about to puke.

"I don't think he wants any," I said, brushing past Preston and setting my trays down on the table. Immediately, a gaggle of children pressed forward and snatched eggs with both hands. I handed out napkins to them as fast as I could but gave up when my small pile ran out. One of their mothers took over, clucking over the group like a broody hen.

"Be careful—don't touch that—you've got some on your cheek—"

Someone tapped on the live microphone, and the sound echoed through the space. I turned to see Doc—in a tuxedo!—standing on the stage. He ran a hand over his combover, cleared his throat, and spoke into the mic as a hush grew over the crowd. "Well, folks. It's time. It's been a pleasure serving as your interim mayor while Margie recovered, but my stint is thankfully over. I'm going to turn the floor over to Marv."

The microphone screeched as Doc awkwardly passed it to

the Marv, the city council chairman who was somehow shaped like a raindrop, with a tall, pointy head, and a large, saggy bottom.

Marv licked his lips nervously. "Let's give a round of applause to Doc for stepping up in a time of need. He did what needed to be done."

The crowd clapped politely and pressed forward a tiny bit toward the stage, anticipating the announcement of the election results. I edged around the side toward the front of the room, meeting eyes with Eli who gave me an encouraging nod from where he was stationed. I knew he'd chosen his position in case the killer made a run for it, but I sure wished he was standing closer to me.

"If the candidates will join me up here?" Marv motioned to Margie and Cal in the front row of audience. They took opposite routes onto the stage to stand behind Marv. Margie's face was a picture of calm confidence, but her hairdo quivered as she stood there with her hands clasped over her pocketbook, giving away her nerves. Cal just looked miserable while he scanned the crowd. Any confidence he'd had as Honeytree's golden boy had been shattered over the last couple of weeks. But his misery did nothing to diminish his All-American good looks. I guessed that his widower status had made him all the more attractive to many single women in town, too, judging by the shiny-eyed adoration many of them were directing toward the stage.

Marv licked his lips again as he unlocked the blue box and carefully withdrew a sealed envelope. "These votes have been triple-counted and verified by the bank manager," he said as he tore open the envelope. "The mayor-elect of Honeytree is… "

For a moment, he struggled to remove the sheet of paper from the envelope, and I thought the room was going to explode with tension. Even I caught myself leaning forward as he unfolded the paper and read the name to himself. His eyebrows raised.

"Calvin Goodbody," Marv finished.

The room erupted with cheers. Margie's fake smile wavered for only a millisecond before she turned to Cal and shook his hand graciously. Doc joined her on stage and helped her down the stairs to the audience. Cal stood awkwardly in place until Preston motioned for him to join Marv at the front of the stage.

Smile, I saw Preston mouth at him, and Cal pasted one on. Well, it was more of a grimace, but he was trying. He leaned over to speak into the mic.

"Thank you to everyone who has supported me through this difficult campaign. I know Amelia is looking down on us from heaven." He kissed his thumb and made a motion toward the ceiling, and the audience renewed their applause.

Well, except Margie. She and Doc were trying to make a hasty exit. I saw Eli step between them and the doorway, blocking their path. I hoped he could keep them in the room long enough for me to do my part.

"If we could get the judge out here for the swearing in?" Marv said into the microphone, scanning the stage behind him. A judge, who'd driven up from Roseburg to do the honors and had been waiting in the wings for his cue, hustled to the mic. As he held out his Bible for Cal to place his hand on, Tammy Jenson sidled up to me.

"Can you believe Margie Morrow got deposed?" she asked, cackling.

"Yeah," I said absentmindedly, my eyes trained on the stage, waiting for my moment.

"Is this the first election she's ever lost? She must be steaming."

"Mhm." I ignored Tammy and watched as Cal held his hand above the Bible, hesitating.

"Go on, son. Place your hand on the good book," the judge urged.

Cal pulled back his hand, clenching it into a fist. From the front row, Preston frowned, his eyes a question mark. He swiftly mounted the steps to stand beside Cal, placing his hand gently on Cal's shoulder.

"Are you OK?"

Cal almost imperceptibly shook his head even as the judge stepped toward him, the Bible still in his outstretched hand.

"Just say the oath, and then we'll figure it out," Preston urged. He picked up Cal's wrist and tried to put his hand on the book, but Cal tensed, jerking his arm out of Preston's grasp.

"I can't do it!" he gasped.

Preston rubbed his forehead. "Why in the *world* not?"

A quick glance at Eli confirmed what I already knew. It was go-time. I stepped forward so I was standing in front of the murmuring crowd. In a loud voice, I said, "I know why not."

The room went silent. Both men turned to look at me.

I took a deep breath. "You're afraid to take an oath on the Bible because you know you betrayed your wife to get here, didn't you?"

Cal's chin began to wobble, and he put his hand over his mouth.

"He did no such thing!" Preston said sharply, looking around at the crowd in a panic.

With deep pain in his eyes, Cal turned to him. "I did, though."

The crowd began buzzing again as people tried to figure out what was going on.

"Leona?" I heard Ruth ask behind me.

I felt terrible about it, but the plan was clearly working, so I kept pressing, raising my voice. "You broke your promise to Amelia. You told her you'd drop out of the race so the two of you could be happy together. But then you didn't."

Preston's eyes went wide. "She died! That's not his fault!"

"Isn't it?" I asked.

Cal's face crumpled. "It is—it is my fault." He shook his head and stumbled back from the mic, holding his head in his hands and mumbling to himself where the microphone couldn't pick up his words.

Preston grabbed the microphone from the stand. "It'll just be a moment while we regroup, folks. He's just overwhelmed. It's been an emotional few weeks." That was the understatement of the year.

"Think about it, Pastor Cal," I said, even louder this time. "Do you even want to be mayor after what happened to Amelia?"

Cal looked at me and back then at Preston. "I don't want to let anybody down," he said slowly.

"That's right!" Preston said, making a coaxing motion like you would at a dog hiding under the bed. "Just come take the oath, and then we'll take a break, I promise." He flashed a smile at the crowd and the judge, who was clutching the Bible to his chest, bewildered at the turn of events.

I checked over my shoulder to see if Eli had been successful at the door. Sure enough, Doc and Marge were still here—and they were *very* interested in what was going on. Marge had found her way back to the front row, and Doc was close behind her, watching over her shoulder.

Cal started back toward the center of the stage and Preston visibly relaxed. "That's right. Just put your hand here and repeat after the nice judge."

"I solemnly swear, in front of God and these witnesses," the judge began.

Cal pulled his hand away again, tears welling in his eyes. "I can't. I'm sorry, Preston." He turned and rushed off the stage and into the audience.

Chapter 27

"Cal!" Preston called to him. "Cal! Please! Stop!"

But Cal didn't listen. He ran straight for the exit where Eli was standing. The crowd parted for him even as people gasped.

"You can't do this!" Preston screeched from the stage. "I won't let you just throw this away for some cheap floozy. You owe me for all I've done to get you here!"

At those words, Cal skidded to a stop and slowly turned back toward the Preston. "And what have you done, exactly?" he asked. After waiting a beat, he strode back through the crowd like Moses through the Red Sea, his shoulders squaring as his usual confidence returned.

Preston's mouth worked as he watched Cal move toward him, his eyes darting around to the exits from the community center. "I—I just did what needed to be done. I took care of the things standing in your way."

"Like my wife?" Cal's voice took on a dangerous edge. "Did you take care of *her*?"

"Amelia wasn't your wife!" Preston said, his voice shrill. "She was just an impediment. You never would have been elected if I hadn't—" He broke off as Cal nearly leaped up the stairs onto the stage.

"Hadn't what?" Cal growled. The crowd hung on his every word. I even found myself holding my breath, even though I knew this moment was coming. I felt rather than saw Eli move toward the stage, too, ready for whatever happened next.

Preston didn't answer.

I cleared my throat and answered for him. "He poisoned her coffee during the church meeting before the Scramble."

The crowd around me gasped. Ruth joined me at the front of the group, clutching my arm apprehensively. "Are you sure?" she murmured.

I gave her a quick nod. It was the most I could do with the amount of adrenaline coursing through my veins. All of my attention was focused on the two men on stage, waiting to see what would happen next. I felt Ruth's hand slip comfortingly into mine and squeeze.

Cal looked green around the gills as he stared at his campaign manager. "Is that true? It *is*, isn't it? I can see it in your face. You wanted her out of the way so I wouldn't drop out of the race."

Preston tightened his jaw and looked away, unwilling or unable to answer Cal's accusation. Cal advanced on him. "You didn't care that I won, though, did you? All of this was about *you* winning. This was never about me becoming the mayor of Honeytree."

Something in Preston snapped. He gave a bitter laugh. "Obviously! Why in the world would I care about some goody-two-shoes pastor becoming the mayor of a tiny town in the middle of nowhere? I'm here to build a reputation—to *rise*. I have real ambition, unlike you. Of course there were going to be some casualties along the way."

"Like Amelia." Cal's eyes burned into Preston.

"Yes, like your so-called *wife*. The woman who loved you so much, she was married to someone else. The woman who loved you so much, she wanted you to live a small life, scraping by as the pastor of a nothing little church." Preston spat the words, and Cal's fists clenched by his sides. He looked ready to strangle Preston right then and there—and might have, if Eli hadn't stepped up between them.

I was so caught up in the moment that I didn't notice Doc had moved up to the edge of the stage until he spoke, his voice ringing out clear and loud. "What about *my* wife, sir? Was she another casualty of your ambition?"

Preston looked Doc up and down and then snorted. "She was a casualty of her own ambition. If she hadn't meddled, I wouldn't have had to poison her, too. It's just a shame she survived so we had to hold this farce of an election. Everyone knows Cal will be a better mayor than *her*." He nodded toward Margie in the front row, whose pale complexion was growing redder by the second.

"He better watch it or Margie's gonna blow," Ruth said under her breath as a wave of chatter swept over the crowd.

I nodded. "The funny thing is, Preston's probably right about Cal and Margie. Cal *would* be a better mayor just because he's less of a bully. She even bullies her own husband."

I watched as Margie's lips quivered, waiting for her to erupt. But to my surprise, it was Doc who lost his temper first. "You spiteful, good-for-nothing, bootlicking backstabber! I wish *you'd* had a sip of your own medicine."

Preston barked a laugh. "I wish you'd had a taste of it, too. You were supposed to—if you and mangy Marge hadn't flounced on the meeting, you'd all have gone down in one terrible, tragic accident." He clasped his hands under his chin

205

and drew his face into a grimace of satirical grief. In a syrupy, sarcastic voice, he said, "I don't know *how* that darn yellow-bellied newt crawled into the coffee pot, Sheriff." He fluttered his eyelashes at Eli.

Eli gave him such a look of disgust that I made a mental note to never flutter my eyelashes again.

Realization dawned on Cal's face. "That's why you made me whiten my teeth that morning—so I couldn't drink the coffee. And you didn't have any yourself, because you knew it was poisoned. It's just lucky that the Morrows weren't killed along with Amelia."

"Not for lack of trying!" Doc added, still steaming in front of the stage.

Cal shook his head sadly as he looked at Preston. All the anger seemed to have drained out of him with Preston's admission. Now he just looked like a limp husk of the man he'd been during the Scramble. "Why didn't I see you for what you were?"

"Nobody could have seen it," Eli said soothingly as he pulled a pair of handcuffs from his belt pouch and motioned for Preston to turn around. "Well, except Leona. She figured it out."

It felt like the whole room turned toward me.

"How *did* you know?" Ruth asked. The folks around her nodded and wondered aloud the same thing.

"It was the coffee," I stuttered, my cheeks flaming due to the unexpected attention. "At the Scramble meeting, Preston said that he didn't drink caffeine, but then later I saw him have a second cup of coffee at the Rx Café. I know for a fact that Sara doesn't serve decaf. Plus, he was eating at the café on Saturday afternoon when nobody else in town would because they were afraid of food poisoning. *He* knew Amelia hadn't been poisoned there, because he was the one who poisoned her. But I didn't know he was trying to kill Margie and Doc, too."

While I was talking, Eli had taken advantage of the distraction and moved around behind Preston to handcuff him. "I guess that's all, folks," he said. He moved to close the first handcuff around Preston's wrist.

But Preston wasn't going gracefully. He tore his hand away from Eli's grasp and dove from the stage, rolling as he landed. Three giant steps and he was face-to-face with me. I froze in fear. He grabbed me by the neck and began to squeeze, his mouth contorted with anger.

"Help!" I squeaked with what breath I had remaining, my hands flailing as uselessly as T-Rex arms. Ruth leaped into action and grabbed his fingers, prying them off one-by-one, but she couldn't work fast enough. Spots swam in front of my eyes and I thought I was going to pass out. I saw a blur behind Preston a millisecond before Doc Morrow tackled him, knocking him off his feet and away from me. I stumbled backward and fell down, coughing and rubbing the searing pain in my throat where Preston's fingers had dug into my skin.

"Are you all right?!" Ruth gasped, kneeling beside me.

"Fine," I croaked. "Actually, better than fine. Look." I nodded to where Eli was handcuffing Preston, with a knee in his back, while Doc Morrow sat on his feet.

"Who knew Doc had it in him?" Ruth said wonderingly.

Margie reached down a hand to help me to my feet. "I did," she said, as she patted the Aqua Net atrocity on her head. "Why do you think I married him?"

Preston didn't even attempt a struggle once he was in cuffs.

He just smiled thinly as Eli read him his rights. I imagined that prison wouldn't be such a bad place for someone with ruthless ambition like Preston's. He'd find a new way to rise, as he put it. New candidates to help to the top of the jailhouse pecking order.

As Eli led Preston toward the exit and the pitch of the crowd's conversation rose, Margie's voice echoed through the community center. "We're not quite done here!"

We all stopped our chatting to look at her. She marched up the stairs of the stage, past the shellshocked judge still clutching his Bible, and went to the microphone. She waved Cal over and waited until he was at her side. Then she motioned the judge over, too. "Come on, boys. We still have an oath to take."

The judge nodded and extended his Bible to Cal again. But Cal shook his head and backed away. "No—no, I can't. I meant what I said earlier. I promised Amelia I'd step back from politics, and I'm going to keep my promise to her."

My heart panged for him. When I'd gone to him in the days before the election and revealed my suspicions about Preston, Cal had confided that he didn't think he could handle the role as mayor, anyway. All he'd ever wanted was to lead his congregation with Amelia by his side. Preston had convinced him that Honeytree needed an ethical, upstanding leader—and we did. But his heart wasn't in it now that Amelia was gone, especially since they'd decided together to quit the campaign.

So he and I came up with the script for confronting Preston—one that required Cal to pretend for one more week that he wanted to be mayor, only to pull back at the last minute—with the hopes that it'd send Preston into a spiral of anger.

Wow, had it worked. But now Honeytree was in a pickle.

The mayor they'd elected didn't want to serve.

Cal gestured to the Bible. "It's all yours, Mayor."

Ruth and I shared a look. Marge-in-Charge was going to be insufferable now that she was mayor again. I hoped she wouldn't hold a grudge against me and Lucky Cluck Farm during her next term. She might never approve my farmers market booth, and if she made another complaint against me to the ODA, I could get shut down completely.

But to everyone's astonishment, mine perhaps the greatest, Margie straightened her gloves and shook her head, too. "No," she said. "I didn't win. I don't want it unless I deserve it. I can't accept the role unless we have another election without any meddling—or murders."

Chatter rippled through the crowd. I could tell everyone was asking the question that was on my mind, too. If not Cal or Margie, who would lead Honeytree?

Marv returned to the stage and patted the judge on the shoulder. "Sorry, buddy. Looks like you're going to have to drive back up here another day. Folks, prepare yourselves. We'll have to hold another election in November. For the next six months, Honeytree will have an interim mayor."

"Doc!" came a shout from the back of the room. Then a few more people called out his name. A second later and a chant began in earnest, Margie joining in and clapping along with it as she stood on stage. "Doc! Doc! Doc!"

Marv held up his hands and the chant died down. He grinned down at the front row where Doc Morrow stood in his tux, which was slightly rumpled after his tussle with Preston. "Doc, if you'll have us?"

Doc hesitated, staring up at his wife on stage. Margie winked at him. "You don't need my permission, Warren. The people have spoken."

Chapter 28

Epilogue, four weeks later

For the second week in a row, the egg coolers in the back of my Suburban were completely empty. The farmers market had turned out to be a stellar way to find customers. I even had a list of pre-orders for next Thursday's market that was as long as my arm. And even better news—Sara was re-opening the Rx Café and had placed a standing weekly order, too.

It was hard to believe that only a month ago, my farm seemed doomed to fail. Now it was doing so well that I could barely keep up. With the egg demand exceeding my current supply, I planned to order a new batch of chicks from the hatchery next week. Lucky Cluck Farm's egg production would double by this time next year. It felt like a fluke, this sudden success, even though I knew it was because of all my hard work—plus a little luck.

I smiled as I thought about my flock waiting patiently for me on the farm. Well, maybe not so patiently. They were probably fussing over being shut up in the run all day. I'd better let them out when I got home, or I might have a mutiny on my hands.

I passed the blueberry farm and noticed that a "sold" placard had been added to the top of the for-sale sign during the time I'd been in town. The deal with Jam and Jelly must have finally closed. I made a mental note to call Ruth and congratulate her—and thank her for the idea to join the farmers market. She'd been too busy to stop by my booth today, but I wanted her to know it was a runaway success.

But before that, I'd pop over and welcome the new neighbors with a dozen eggs. Maybe if I got them addicted to the rich yellow yolks, they'd go easier on me when I dug in my heels and refused to tear down my chicken palace. I crossed my fingers as I parked and jumped out to grab an empty egg carton from the back of the car. There weren't any eggs left in the porch fridge, so I hoped my girls laid a few while I was at the market.

The hinges on the door to the nest boxes creaked as I peered inside. A beautiful sight greeted my eyes: at least two dozen eggs had been laid in my absence. I selected the prettiest, smoothest ones to add to the carton for Jam and Jelly. As I moved down the line, swiping a couple of eggs from each box, Dr. Speckle muttered at me from her spot in the rightmost nest box and hunched up her feathers.

"Oh, no you don't!" I pushed her off the nest and collected the three eggs she'd been trying to incubate. I knew the early signs of a broody hen when I saw them. She stalked off, muttering and rearranging her feathers. Hopefully being evicted this early would cure her of her motherly intentions. I wanted more chicks, to be sure, but I didn't want more broody hens, and the old timers at the feed store had warned me that it was catching.

With a full carton of freshly laid eggs in hand, I squeezed through the barbed-wire fence that separated my apple orchard from the blueberry farm next door and headed up the row of bushes toward the white farmhouse. I could make out a couple of cars parked up there, so I knew my new neighbors were home.

As I neared, I noticed one of the cars was Ruth's. She was probably there for the same reason I was—to congratulate the buyers. I waved and called a greeting to the people standing on the porch before I realized who they were. Ruth was there, of course, but Eli was standing behind her at the door, too. A whole welcoming committee.

Interesting.

"Hey, Leona," Eli said, grinning at me over the top of Ruth's head. "How's it going?"

I held up the eggs as I glanced around for Jam and Jelly. "Good. Just saw the 'sold' sign and came over to welcome the new neighbors."

"Perfect timing." Ruth flashed a huge smile at me as she jingled a key. "Your new neighbor was just moving in."

To my surprise, she handed the key to Eli, and he used it to unlock the front door. I frowned. "Are Jam—I mean, Sam and Kelly meeting you here?"

"Nope," Ruth said.

Eli glanced impatiently over his shoulder from the doorway. "Come on in. What do you think? Should I store those eggs in the fridge?"

He was acting like he owned the place.

Wait a minute—Ruth had handed the keys to him.

And—I glanced over my shoulder to double-check the driveway—Jam and Jelly were nowhere in sight.

Was this really happening? *Did Eli buy the blueberry farm?*

I pinched myself in that tender spot on my upper arm. Nope.

Not a dream.

Motherclucker.

"Your face!" Ruth pointed at me and started cracking up. She laughed so hard she bent over with her hands on her knees, tears streaming down her face.

"Glad you're entertained by my ignorance," I snapped, walking past her into the farmhouse's little vintage kitchen. Eli was leaned up against the fridge, his arms crossed and his eyes crinkled with amusement. I sucked in my cheeks as I set the eggs on the counter. "Did you really buy this farm?"

"Yup."

"What?! How? And more importantly, *why?*"

"I'm sorry I didn't tell you." He stretched out his hands beseechingly.

"He's been shopping for a while," Ruth said behind me.

Eli nodded. "I've always wanted a little piece of property. Been saving since my military days, actually. I thought I'd buy a place when I had a wife and kids, but that just never happened, so I never pulled the trigger. But then you came back to town, doing this farming thing all on your own, and I was like—what am I waiting for?"

I blinked. "I see. And you thought you'd move in next door to me?"

"No, he *didn't* want to move in next door," Ruth interjected.

Eli shrugged. "I worried it'd be weird."

"It is a little weird," I said, nodding.

"That's why Ruth and I've been shopping around so much. I was hoping another property would come up that I liked better. But honestly, this place is perfect—it's exactly what I've always wanted. Including its proximity to you," he finished, color rising on his neck for an awkward beat. Then he rushed

214

to add, "But that's just the icing on the cake. I really did try and find somewhere else so you wouldn't feel like I was breathing down your neck. I know you like your space."

I whirled on Ruth. "How'd you get out of selling it to Jam and Jelly? Didn't you have to present their offer to the seller?"

"Yes, I did," she said, her eyes twinkling. "You made sure of that, you brat. There was only one way I could stop you from making the worst mistake of your life, and that was to present a competing offer. That's where Eli came in. He's your knight in shining armor. He saved you from living next door to Jam and Jelly for the next twenty years."

Eli beamed. "When Ruth told me it was me or them, I figured I was the better option. So I pulled the trigger and put in an offer at the same time they did. I don't think I'm bragging when I say I have the most to offer."

I rolled my eyes at his bad joke, but I can't say I disagreed.

Ruth chimed in. "We've been dying to tell you—it's been so hard not to spill the beans when you're around that we've both been avoiding you a little."

Now that, I'd noticed. I'd chalked it up to some budding romantic interest between them that they didn't want everyone to know about yet. I motioned between them. "So you two aren't...?"

Ruth laughed. "No! Gross!"

Eli pulled a face at her. "I'm not that gross. But we're just friends, if that's what you're asking. Poor Ruth's had a certain high-maintenance real estate client monopolizing her every spare minute. But now that I've found my forever home, maybe she'll have time to date. Maybe I will, too." He gave me a very saucy wink.

My knees felt a little weak. For lack of a chair to sit on, I slid down the cabinets to the kitchen floor. Eli's kitchen floor. "Why all the secrecy, then? You should have just told me!"

Ruth plopped down beside me and put her arm around my shoulder. "Because you would have tried to sabotage it, you silly goose. You would have done everything short of cut off your right arm to stop Eli from buying this place."

She was right. I would have—but it wasn't because I was a goose. It was because I was chicken. Straight-up scared of what it might mean if I let the sparks between me and Eli turn into something more. And fear was a terrible reason to give up on something.

Ruth struggled to her feet and offered me a hand. I let her help me up and then gave her a tight hug. "You can thank me later," she murmured in my ear. "Are you mad at me?"

I couldn't answer. My throat was tight, my heart welling over with emotion. Yes, I was mad—but not mad at her for hiding this from me. I was mad at myself for being so stubborn that I always got in my own way. Lucky for me, my friends knew me better than I knew myself. They'd protect me from all enemies, whether that enemy was an overambitious campaign manager with a penchant for poison, or just myself. I blinked away my tears and shook my head.

"Good. I'm glad." She patted my hand and looked past me to Eli. "Welcome home, Eli."

"Thanks, Ruth. I'll have you over for dinner when I get the kitchen unpacked." He smiled awkwardly at me once she'd left. "You're invited, too. Every night, if you want."

I grimaced, and he laughed out loud. "What, it sounds that bad? I'll have you know that I'm a pretty decent cook. I'm a big boy, Leona. I even wash my own socks."

I shook my head. "No, it doesn't sound bad at all. You're

telling me I've got a man next door who'll build me a chicken coop, forgive my speeding tickets, and cook me dinner...and he goes back to his own home every night and does laundry? How can I resist?"

He pulled me into his arms and planted the best, Doublemintiest kiss of my life on me. In that moment, I gave up on protecting my heart from Eli Ramirez. If it killed me, it killed me, but at least it'd be a good death.

Read More

Want to read more in the Clucks and Clues Cozy Mystery Series? Visit www.hillaryavis.com to see the full list of titles, download free ebooks, sign up for email updates, and more!

About the Author

Hillary Avis lurks and works in beautiful Eugene, Oregon, with her very patient husband and a menagerie of kids, cats, dogs, and chickens. When she's not thinking up amusing ways to murder people, she makes pottery, drinks coffee, and streams *The Great British Bake-Off*, but not all at the same time.

Hillary is the author of cozy mysteries about smart women who uncover truths about themselves, their communities, and of course any unsolved crimes they happen to stumble across. You can read more about her and her work at www.hillaryavis.com.